MAX

The Tale of a Waggish Dog

This story reflects the life of a real dog.
Its human characters, though, are not to be identified with any persons, living or dead.

Paul Bennett

Mayhaven Publishing

Mayhaven Publishing
P O Box 557
Mahomet, Illinois 61853
U S A

Cover Art by: Loren Kirkwood

First Edition - First Printing 1999
Library of Congress Catalog Number: 98-67051
ISBN 1-878044-64-8

Dedication

For Dogs
and
All Who Love Them

Especially
Charlie and Ida
Bill and Lisa
and
Christina, Lindsay, Michael, Steven, Kittery

Other Books by Paul Bennett

Fiction:

Robbery on the Highway

The Living Things

Follow the River

Poetry:

A Strange Affinity

The Eye of Reason

Building a House

The Sun and What it Says Endlessly

Appalachian Mettle

To Max

You galloped through our Granville lives.

Oh, womanizer you, with tales of roaming
and testing belief for sense acuity.

Steam in windows, Dad needs food.
Wait, the door will move.

Check the tag, find the number—
No more the call to Burg.

Max is home.

—June Kraus

Contents

“There ain’t no harm in a hound, nohow.”

—Huck Finn

The life story of our dog Max would not please my father, were he alive to read it. Father was a severe man of the cloth of Irish-English ancestry, the product of three institutions of higher learning. His middle name—Emerson—seemed to have strangled his Irish sense of humor in the crib, even as it distanced him from mankind and animals throughout his life. Not only did he assume that men and women are to be closely supervised—even herded—from the cradle to the grave, and children seldom seen and never heard, but he believed dogs are born curs to be cuffed and kicked at will.

That my wife Jeanne and I—once our two sons were grown and gone to homes of their own—attached ourselves as parents to a dog, Father would have termed “shite,” which was as close as he came to four-letter cursing. But Jeanne and I regarded Max as the fortunate child of our old age, and regularly we fell into such language as “Max, come with Mommy, come with Daddy” as we tried to guide our beautiful 75-pound black and tan child past life’s obstacles. And “guide” itself took on a strange frisky meaning when Jeanne and I—for better or worse, as the vow has it—found ourselves trailing Max from one escapade to another, never quite sure who held the leash, who wore the collar. What happened during an afternoon's excursion to the local IGA Store for our weekly stash of groceries will clarify my meaning.

The IGA Store lies at the center of a black-topped field on the bank of Raccoon Creek just south of the town of Granville, Ohio, home of Denison University, where I teach in the English Department. Friday afternoon traffic cluttered Granville as we coaxed our stall-prone ten year old station wagon through the stoplight and south on Main Street to the store parking lot. Moving at our uncertain pace, Jeanne and I in the front seat, Max at the back window riding shotgun on our rear as he liked to do in enemy territory, I became aware that we were being overtaken by the one Rolls-Royce in Granville. The Rolls—a "Silver Cloud"—we had beheld from time to time at a distance, sailing over hill and dale, but we had never met its immaculately dressed driver, regarding him with the awe reserved for those who speed through life on gossamer wings.

Now, seeing "Cloud Nine," as the license aptly identified the Silver Cloud, floating in my rear view mirror and seeing only one parking place relatively near the IGA front door, I kept our stumbling station wagon on course as the other driver and I eyed the privileged parking place. Although I held a slight advantage on the turn, at the last moment I braked and passed up the parking spot, and steered our wagon toward an anchorage in the boondocks.

Jeanne, who had not been aware of the noiseless gleaming cloud shadowing us, shot me a quizzical "Why?"

Her query became "Oh, I see," as "Cloud Nine" swished in to occupy the privileged parking place.

Max, who had been shotgunning with only one eye open, sensed a confrontation—his parents being put upon—opened both eyes and raised his dome-shaped head. Spotting the Silver Cloud he shook out his umbrella houndish ears and gave a sniff and growl, then a trancing stare, followed by a groan.

His growl may or may not have been intended for the stranger, but his attenuated groan was plainly meant for me. Worse yet, I saw that the grey-haired senatorial man at the wheel of "Cloud Nine" had leaped from his throne and was headed not for the store but straight for our station wagon. Perplexed and fearful that my driving or demeanor or mien had somehow offended our affluent fellow townsman, I whispered to Jeanne: "Do you know—"

"Never saw him," Jeanne breathed, "I mean *met*. Could he be somebody you have met at the college?"

"Never. Not that I can—"

The radiant stranger was upon us, setting his alligator shoes down purposefully, but *ignoring* Jeanne and me. His hand thrust out and he smiled. "Max! Max, old boy, how are you?"

Max, who had bounded from the rear to the middle seat, sat upright, cool, collected, but with his tail nodding ever so slightly as he accepted the manicured hand on his head.

The smiling stranger turned to Jeanne and me. "I'm Harvey Roundsdale; I operate the Zane Trail Raceway." As we shook hands, he explained: "Your Max and I are old friends.

He was out to our house at Briar Hill the other evening, stood up at our dining window and watched us all the time we ate dinner. After dinner he came to the front door and we got acquainted. He played catch the tennis ball with Mrs. Roundsdale and me for some time and then went along." He reached out and clicked the tag on Max's choke collar—quoted it from memory: "Max, West Burg Street, Granville, Ohio. Call my dad: 555-2135." Again his hand moved to Max's head, lingered to finger a silken ear.

Max, sensing that he had handled a testy situation, nudged the well-groomed hand that now tugged at his ear. Turning to embrace Jeanne and me, he let out an extra inch of red tongue and flashed his pearly half-inch canines.

"Some dog, he's some dog!" Harvey Roundsdale exclaimed as he stepped back.

"He's always surprising us," I said.

"He's brought us more friends, more experiences—" Jeanne added as our new acquaintance, brushing back his hair and straightening his tie, moved off. From a distance he exclaimed:

"Max, you're some dog—some dog!"

Just a Pup

He was one of a litter of ten pups born in a barrel of straw on a farm outside Newark, Ohio, during a howling snowstorm on December 15, 1977. The blowing snow and bitter winds of that vile December night were but a foretaste of the great blizzard that settled in and paralyzed the Midwest—and Ohio in particular—throughout the winter of '77-78. Born when and where they were, it was only by God's grace that he and his nine brothers and sisters survived the blizzard, a blizzard that Governor James Rhodes of Ohio characterized—one of his few correct calls, I might add—as "A killer storm looking for victims."

The pup's parentage fulfilled the prescription of our old family doctor who was fond of saying—even repeating, when he'd had one cup too many: "An attending doctor can always be sure of one parent: the mother."*His* mother was a German shepherd of noble German lineage all duly spelled out in the American Kennel Club record books. His father was—well, the Newark *Advocate* named him "farm collie," but one could only be sure he was some visiting fireman who had met and run with the noble German shepherd bitch on moonlit hunts over the hills of Licking County in the fall of 1977. (I'll have more to say on this putative father later.)

Not only was his mother AKC registered, she was almost too beautiful to believe. Light tan in color, of regal bearing despite the prominence of her every rib, she seemed to Jeanne and me as we mused upon her German heritage that she had to be the Greta Garbo of her canine clan: classic the lines of her nose, ears, and head; trim and shapely her frame and carriage; long and graceful her legs. Of course we did not see her in the throes of birth, did not behold her at all until we stood in the winter chill well beyond the reach of her heavy chain as she barked threats at us and commands to her straying offspring that February afternoon in 1978.

Standing on the wind-swept grass-covered slope below the chained mother and her many sons and daughters, Jeanne and I had no notion of what we were looking for in a dog. In fact, we weren't too sure we were there to do more than look, but Valentine's Day was in the offing and we had yet to get a valentine. From some fifty feet we studied the ten undernourished pups—nine were tan or buff or brown, one was black; some had longish ears, some had short. Long we stood and pondered.

Finally I said to Jeanne: "If you were to take one, which would it be?"

"Good question," Jeanne said.

While we hesitated, attempting to single out this or that pup in the melee, three of them detached themselves from the gamboling herd and ran aslant the hill in an ear-tugging game of chase—one buff, one tan, and the black. Jeanne and I squatted and gave forth what we meant to be welcoming sounds. Simultaneously the three lean and hungry players caught sight of us, heard our pleas, and spilled down the slope toward us. First to arrive was the black—then the buff, then the tan. The black headed to Jeanne, and she caught him up in her hands, even as I lifted the tan—the buff had at the last minute turned tail and retreated to her mother.

Jeanne and I each stood with a pup in our hands, maneuvering to let the pup ride an arm, and I said:

"Assuming these two selected us—which would it be?"

"Look at this," Jeanne said. The black had begun mouthing her fingers and as he did so had exposed his tongue. Then I saw what Jeanne was pointing to: a severe cut half-way across the pink tongue.

"He probably got that cut trying to lick nourishment out of a broken bottle," I said. "Look at this." The tan, who appeared a bit better nourished than the black, had settled across my arm and was closing his eyes as I stroked him. "This is the contented kid, the happy one," I said.

Jeanne held up the black with the deeply notched tongue and said, "I'd take the dark one. He's the hungry one, the one who chose us first, the one who just might need us. Besides, he's got his private hurt, his mark. We'd know him anywhere."

Jeanne and I had been married long enough that I know when she's on a roll, when her womanly intuition is running with full-moon power. "What would you name him?" I asked.

Jeanne bent to the little face smiling hopefully up at her. "I'd name him—" she paused but an instant—"Max."

"Max it is; he's the one!" I said. And I carried the contented tan a few steps toward his mother and set him down—nudged him toward the litter.

To my surprise Jeanne did the same with the black—with *Max.* The two pups ran to their mother. Max, plainly the dash-man of the litter, got there first. The mother received him, sniffed and mouthed him, turned him on his back and gave him a few finishing licks, and turned away.

Jeanne knelt and snapped her fingers, gave her own mothering whimper. Max looked at her, let his tail twitch, then looked at *his* mother. His mother was receiving the tan I had held, wiping the stranger's taint off him.

Max hesitated—what was he thinking?—then turned toward Jeanne and ran to her.

"You've got a valentine," I suggested. "His mother just bade him goodbye."

"I chose the dark one, I've got a Max," Jeanne said as she raised the black pup with the longish ears, domed shaped head and cushioned him against her breast.

Moments later I stood knocking on the door of the lean-to back section of the ancient farmhouse, and Jeanne stood by my side with Max in her arms, snuggling deeper under her heavy wool coat to avoid the wind. I thought back to the telephone conversation that had brought us to this farm on Sleepy Hollow Road.

On the telephone the working housewife who owned the thoroughbred German shepherd bitch—fixed forever in our memories as Max's mother—had sounded desperate. The existence of the non-registered and non-registerable litter of pups was—she said—a complete disaster. Not only had she been forced to mid-wife the litter into this world and care for them throughout the blizzard, but now the pups, nearly two months of age and getting too leggy to sell, were eating her out of house and home. "I'd be more'n glad not to have to deliver them to the Pound. I'd be more'n glad to have them go to a good home for free. You'd be welcome to one *or* the litter."

"Your advertisement said they'd be ten dollars each," I responded.

"I was thinkin' of askin' that but—"

Our conversation moved back and forth like a skit played out in eighteenth century Philadelphia between two competing gurus: Titan Leeds and Benjamin Franklin. Leeds in his almanac offered this version: "Necessity is a mighty weapon." Franklin in his Poor Richard's Almanac this more stylish version: "Necessity never made a good bargain." Franklin was the better stylist, the sharper dealer, and had driven his competitor out of business.

My repeated knocking on the farmhouse door brought forth a gray-haired elderly man, clad in khaki trousers and a worn red flannel shirt. He stepped through the sticking door and pulled it shut after him.

"You're the owner of the pups?" I asked.

"I'm the step-father. My step-daughter's off at work today," he said. "I see you picked out one of the pups."

"The dark one," Jeanne said. "We plan to call him Max."

"Well," the man shivered and turned toward the door.

"You're more'n welcome to him." His hand was on the knob.

"Would—would this be all right?" I asked, holding out a ten-dollar bill.

The man hesitated. "You wouldn't need to—" He was reaching for the bill. "That's just fine—she'll be pleased—I heard her on the phone to you. She'll be pleased."

"We're the ones who are pleased," I said. "You're sure that's enough?"

"I'm sure," he said. He leaned his shoulder to the door. Again it stuck, then creaked open unevenly. He stepped inside, pulled, yanked, and the door, complaining, shut behind him.

"Franklin would have done it cheaper—with panache," I said to Jeanne as we headed toward our car parked at the end of the rutted lane. "But I don't recall that he ever bought a dog."

"Wasn't he called the father of our country?" Jeanne asked.

"He was—before the title was bestowed upon George Washington," I said. "How'd you know?"

"I knock around a bit, read a bit," Jeanne explained to the dark face on her left shoulder. She turned to me: "You'll be known as the father of our Max."

"I don't think Franklin ever bought a dog," I repeated.

"Never one like this," Jeanne whispered into a dark ear. "Never a Max."

Jeanne and I had acquired title to Max, our task was to make him ours.

On the eight mile drive to our house he let us know we had robbed him of his all: cider-barrel home and dearly loved Mother and Sisters and Brothers. Jeanne's promise of a new home he would love—where he would in turn be loved—went for naught, and the whines that filled the car, had we been able to record and transcribe them, would have been for orphaned children what *Hamlet* is for young men and women, what *Lear* is for the elderly.

Steadily stroking his silken head and ears and playing her fingers down the prominent ribs that rose and fell with his every complaint of our wrong-doing, Jeanne went so far as to say it: "How much we have to learn from you, Max."

Something in her words or tone reached him. Max stopped his keening and lifted and twisted his head in what we were to discover was his personal way of saying "Right on! I'm listening, I really am."

"Well," I said, "I never—'

"Max, Maxie," Jeanne exclaimed to the inquiring face with red-notched tongue that stretched to touch her nose.

"Max," I said, in my natural professorial best, "I hope you'll return the favor by trying to learn something from us." For some reason my voice didn't do its office, for we arrived at West Burg Street, in Granville on a tide of puppy wails and accusations the least of which was blasphemous.

Lessons Learned

Housebreaking Max was what those with street smarts would name "a piece of cake." Unfortunately in February of that bizzare winter of 1978 the piece of cake came with a frigid icing that required Jeanne and me to dress in full winter garb every time we made a run to Max's toilet, which we soon named the training station. But we knew well the basic law of puppy physics: outflow equals input, and the sooner the better if one wishes to keep a house a home.

So, after every feeding—and we started with warm milk and a generous ration of Puppy Chow within minutes of Max's arrival at his new home—he got set astride Jeanne's or my arm to be carried to his training station. The station lay in the shadows of a white pine woods about a hundred yards from the house at the end of the garden. There the ground was covered with three or four inches of snow, topped by a crust of snow-crystals, an ideal, if slippery, puppy privy.

And for as long as it would take Max to learn continence, Jeanne and I agreed we'd make that hundred yard trip after every feeding, and every three or four hours day and night. There may be better ways to housebreak pups, but ours was the Harvard Graduate School Puppy Training Technique—HGSPTT, for short—a system we had developed and put to the acid—friends said *urine*—test in the spring of 1946 when we were residents in a second-floor, living-room bed-room shared-kitchen apartment on Forest Street in Cambridge, Massachusetts. At the time I was a full-time graduate student and teaching assistant and Jeanne was a full-time working wife in Cruft Laboratories as Harvard, and we took upon ourselves the task of housebreaking a five week old collie pup. As to the success of HGSPTT, though it came within hours of breaking Jeanne and me, the collie pup never had a single accident, not one, and he was perfectly housebroken within two weeks.

I am a night person able to get by on very little sleep, a gene-given calibration I found useful during Navy watches in World War II, and Jeanne is very much a day person, so I launched Max on his HGSPTT by taking him to his training station throughout the first night and waiting until the law of puppy physics ran its natural course. During that first night the law itself got tested: outflow appeared to exceed input, possibly due to a kindly stroking with hands and words and Max's desire to please. When Max and I returned to the house triumphant in the morning sun, the after-every-meal and every-three hours or so, HGSPTT was well underway.

You will ask did HGSPTT work? It worked like a habit William James himself might have supervised. Max was no dummy—indeed, as Jeanne and I quickly learned, he was something of an Einstein or at least, honoring his German heritage, *ein kluger Hund.* And as anyone who knows dogs will tell you, dogs—even puppies—delight in keeping their quarters clean, much preferring to leave their signatures and scents at the outermost limits of their ranging territory.

That Max was one smart pup, capable of co-authoring and acting in a drama of the north—dare we call it a Jack London playlet?—was shown by an occurrence of the following week. That occurrence took place on a blustery day when I was at school and Jeanne had dressed in her snowboots and red winter coat and red woolen scarf and white toboggan and white mittens to take Max on his after-lunch "trip." Although I missed the first performance, I got to attend the drama twice that night, in dress rehearsal at the dinner table and then in an on-the-road performance relayed via long distance telephone to our son Bill in Wesfield, Massachusetts.

Here is "The Housebreaking" co-authored by Max and Jeanne:

Jeanne: (talking fast): PB and I are taking turns in housebreaking our valentine pup Max. PB does the night watch and I the day, so every two or three hours I dress in snowboots, winter coat, scarf, toboggan and mittens, and march out to Max's privy.

Bill: I hope you take Max along.

Jeanne: Of course I do, silly. He rides my arm. Anyhow—

Bill: You dressed for that rendezvous as if it were an assignation.

Jeanne: Don't kid Max's mother. Anyhow, I got dressed right after lunch and made the trip. It took some waiting in the cold wind but it worked.

Bill: (laughing) Max worked, you waited.

Jeanne: I stood by and froze. Anyhow, I decided on the way back to the house to go by the mailbox to get the mail—two chores with one trip.

Bill: Two birds with Ein-stein is the cliche.

Jeanne: Did it ever turn out to be one stone! I decided to get the mail while I was dressed for it. It's windy, the snow is blowing, and I had gathered this wad of mail and had it in one mittened hand and Max in the other, when I saw the neighbor—

Bill: Mr. Zimmer?

Jeanne: Yes, Mr. Z himself. He was coming out to get his mail, and I decided he ought to know we had Max. Just know we had a new pup so he could keep an eye on Wolfgang. He's such a big and fierce and unpredictable German shepherd—

Bill: That description fits Wolfgang—but go on, I'm listening.

Jeanne: Yes, So just to let Mr. Z know we had Max and he might need to keep an eye on Wolfgang I decided to show Max to Mr. Z. Slipping and sliding and holding onto Max and the mail I descended on Mr. Z at his mailbox.

Bill: He probably thought it a belated Christmas visit from Saint Jeanne herself.

Jeanne: I got there and stopped, fighting to keep my balance on the slippery road, with Max in one mittened hand and the other full of mail. I began talking to Mr. Z and trying to hold Max out for him to pet. Then the first thing I knew Max reached up a paw quick as a flash and hooked my toboggan, pulled it right down over my eyes. Then Mr. Z began to laugh and tried to help me with Max and the toboggan, and right before I could get the damned toboggan back in place he kissed me right in the mouth—his tongue through my teeth—on mine.

Bill: Mr. Zimmer did that?

Jeanne: Oh my God, no. Max! Max did that! With his tongue, and I was standing there feeling like an utter fool. Wearing those mittens, trying to get the toboggan out of my eyes, trying to keep hold of Max, trying not to drop the mail, and Mr. Z was guffawing. Now you're laughing—What're you laughing at?

Bill: Wait till I tell Charlie about this—you and Mr. Zimmer—

Jeanne: You wouldn't dare! That didn't happen. Bill, you just quit that. I'll never tell you—

Bill: (laughing hilariously) Another—Max—story!

Insight

However clumsy or deft his movement in yanking Jeanne's toboggan over her eyes, Max performed like a straight-A student in basic toilet training. He mastered HGSPTT in twelve days and never once soiled house or car. His favorite sleeping spot—between our twin beds—remained as clean as can be, as did the countless motel rooms he visited through the years.

But in his toilet training one additional bit of learning occurred that neither Jeanne nor I understood at that time: Max learned that the only fit toilet is a snowbank. This bit of learning—and Max could be stubborn about what he knew he knew—presented a slight problem when we journeyed south to Venice, Florida, in March during the college's spring vacation, to attend the Easter Day wedding of my nephew.

Jeanne and I in the front seat, Max on the plaid blanket we'd spread on the rear, we set out to drive from Granville, Ohio, to Venice, Florida, on a sunny Friday morning in March, 1978. Remnants of winter ice and snow lingered in the deep shade on northern slopes, but the road was clear as we sped happily west on Ohio 161 toward Interstate 71, a route that would take us to Cincinnati. In Cincinnati we'd pick up Interstate 75 for Lexington, Kentucky, and points south.

We made a brief stop at an IGA store in New Albany, where we bought a hand of bananas, favorite on-the-road snack for the great ape who drove Max's bus. Once I had my bananas safely stowed, I let Max out, thinking it wise to make sure he was freshly drained for the long morning drive—we hoped to make it to Lexington for a late lunch. Max was now four months of age, and about the size of a beagle, but more legs than body. Freed on the grass at the edge of the IGA parking lot he cast about all around the car, lingering in puzzlement on the shady side, and then set off in a ground-eating lope around the store and across the parking lot at the rear, where a large bread truck was being unloaded. I set out after him.

He ran around the truck, appearing disappointed even disoriented when he came to its northern side. Then he spotted the moving legs of the delivery men. Just as he overtook the uniformed legs—for what purpose I didn't inquire—I overtook him, and got him on his leash and casually walked him off into the grass. He sniffed and looked around—again appearing disappointed—and turned and pulled me around the store to the car.

"Well?" Jeanne asked.

"No luck," I said. "We'll have to try him later on."

"I wonder how he'll travel," Jeanne said.

"We'll soon find out," I said.

"I wonder how he'll react to the traffic in Cincy," Jeanne added.

"I was thinking the same thing," I said. "We'll see."

And we did see, for Max settled down on his plaid blanket, stretched out on his side so that his head rested in the slanting spring sunshine that streamed in on the driver's side of the car, and slept like a stone all the way from Columbus to Cincinnati. As we crossed the Ohio River into Kentucky I looked at Jeanne and we exchanged nods that said "Let sleeping dogs—" On we drove through the greening bluegrass hills and fields rimmed with the white fences of the famous horse farms surrounding Lexington. We arrived at the Holiday Inn south of Lexington at 2:15 p.m; and I parked at the farthest edge of the parking lot near an open field.

"Ideal," Jeanne said.

"Here, Max. Here's your chance," I said, as I opened the door. He got up, front end first, stretched long and luxuriously and slowly climbed down. I snapped the leash in place and we set off into the open field. We walked here and we walked there—Max stopping every now and then, then lunging ahead on the leash; then we ran—he loped, I trotted—across the field and around the field. No go. Finally, we returned to the car—and Max stood gazing into the distance, his umbrella ears at a tilt, his body on point.

"No luck." Jeanne announced. "Is he a camel?"

"You saw it," I said.

"Good exercise," Jeanne mused.

"For the great ape?" I asked.

"For both of you,"

"Do you suppose I'd dare let him loose—he's got to find some way to go," I said.

"It's worth a try."

I reached down and unsnapped the leash. Max looked

up at me before turning to survey the field we had worked over so diligently. Then he whirled and set off in his distancing lope, straight for the main entry of the Holiday Inn. I set off after him but he quickly outdistanced me. He came to the front door of the Inn, which faced us and the parking lot on the south side. He continued on around the building—out of sight. I picked up my speed and rounded the corner. There against the brick wall was Max squatting on a two foot rim of snow that had lingered in the northern shade cast by the building. Plainly he was contributing his mite to the fertility of Kentucky, and as I exclaimed, he finished that number and stooped anew in puppy fashion to begin painting the snow a sulfurous hue.

When we got back to the car, I announced to Jeanne: "When you have to go, you go on snow—Max's motto." Then I explained what I had beheld. "Some pup!" I complimented Max, who was now lolling on the plaid blanket. "You've got a mind of your own and you know where you do your best work," I added.

"Has it crossed *your mind* we're headed for Florida and your pup has just desecrated the last spot of snow south of the Mason-Dixon line?" Jeanne asked dryly.

I was tempted to say we'd cross that bridge when the floods came but I thought better of it. Max was already stretched out on his plaid, and I myself was ready to test the indoor plumbing of the Holiday Inn.

Late that March night the guests in a motel outside Nashville, Tennessee, must have thought they had a peeping Tom on the loose—a blind peeping Tom being led by a straining leggy black and tan pup—for Max and I explored every angle and shadowed nook of that motel, not once but three or four times, before the call of nature got the better of principle, and he settled for a spot of grass under a pine tree, a spot of grass liberally dressed with pine needles.

That episode caused me to tell Jeanne to keep her fingers crossed for transference: that lob-lolly pines might substitute for white pines, that Venice, Florida's white beach sand might substitute for snow.

Looking back I now label Max's search for a snow toilet instinctual and right. How instinctual and right was to be his every action I had no way of knowing at the time, although time—and timing— seemed a part of everything he did, all the crazy, fun things that led Jeanne and me down paths we would never have set foot on but for his showing us Max's way. Max's way in Venice, Florida, led me right smack into someone else's motel room—and there's a story.

It was exactly 4 p.m. when we crossed the bridge into Venice proper and turned left a couple blocks and left again to our motel. Later I was to remember not merely the time but the pleasant feel of the bright Florida sun on my arm, a warmth that served to link me—the banana eater—to the coconut palms lining the street we drove along. then in no time at all we were parked and I had checked in, and I came whistling across the tarmac to the car, jingling the brass key at the end of the red plastic tab stamped Room 8.

"How's that for guessing?" I asked Jeanne, flashing the room tab—we had parked directly in front of our room.

"You're living right," Jeanne said.

"We're all living right," I said to the smiling Max as I opened his door to let him set his padded feet on the State of Florida.

I was leaning over, digging for the leash under my jacket on the floor of the back seat, when Jeanne exclaimed "Hurry!"

"Wh—what?" I straightened.

Max was nowhere to be seen. At first I assumed he had dashed around the car or under it, then I saw where Jeanne pointed. He was on a beeline run for the door of Room 4, a door that stood slightly ajar, and as I stared helplessly, the shadowy outline of his liquid black body nosed through the door and disappeared.

"Max! Max!" I called. "Oh my God."

"Go get him!" Jeanne directed.

I was on the way to the door when it clicked shut. I looked back at our car. Jeanne motioned me on.

Feeling small enough to crawl through the keyhole I stood at Door 4 and knocked. No answer. I knocked again, my mouth at the ready with apology piled on apology.

Then the door swung wide and I found myself staring upon a doorway filled with an American Indian, the kind that had lined the inside cover of my seventh grade history book: deep-chested, tall, long black hair, body carried like a taut bow.

"Excuse me, forgive me," I began, "but our pup just entered your room—"

"You own that pup?" The broad chest resonated like a war-drum. As I listened, dumb-founded, the drum beat on: "You come right in, you come right in. Anyone who owns that pup is a friend of mine. I grew up with Black and Tans. Yes sir. I grew up in North Carolina with Black and Tan hounds and if that's your pup you're my friend.

I felt myself being escorted—drawn—into the darkened rom in which I could see nothing, coming from the bright sunlight.

"I'm Chief Leaping Bear, a Cherokee out of North Carolina. And you're my friend if you own that pup—"

In the shadow I sensed Max was moving toward me—standing much taller than he had stood in the sunlight. For a moment I could have sworn *his* face was at my eye level and his notched tongue was out, his canines exposed in a smile.

"I'm Max's father," I finally managed. "I'm from Ohio. My pup is named Max." I was pumping the outthrust hand—and a terribly strong hand it was.

"I like that name, it's like Stone or Stick," Chief Leaping Bear said. In the shadow he was stooping, whispering "Max, Max!" Then he was on his feet, his hand on my arm, and he was introducing me to a beautiful tall woman who had emerged from the deep shadows. "Blue Star, this is Max Father."

Her teeth were flashing, she was nodding, and for a moment her hands lingered on mine, right and left, then she had crouched down and was caressing Max.

"You're my friend, Max Father," Leaping Bear said. "If you own this pup you've got to be all right. What do you do for a living? I work in metal. I make these—" He motioned towards the wall and Blue Star got up to touch the lamp by the bed.

Suddenly we stood in a gallery, the room shown round with gleaming art work: stars, trees, fish, animals, fanciful abstracts. Most gave off the dull sheen of black metal, several the shine of silver.

Blue Star had knelt to Max and I could see his notched

tongue washing her hands.

"Max Father, what do *you* do?" Leaping Bear repeated.

"I teach at a college in Ohio," I explained.

"He teaches—he's a teacher," Leaping Bear announced to Blue Star. She nodded, her dark eyes shining.

"What is your subject?" Leaping Bear asked.

"I teach writing, American literature, poetry. It's a very small college," I explained.

"Max Father teaches poetry," Leaping Bear exclaimed to Blue Star. "You hear that, he teaches poetry." Leaping Bear thrust both his hands to Blue Star and drew her to her feet. Then he drew himself up to his full height, swinging his right arm around Blue Star, the left around me, joining the two of us, facing us one to the other. "Blue Star is a poet," he said.

"Here." He quickly reached for a chair and motioned me into it. "You sit down right here. Max Father, you sit down right here and Blue Star will read her poetry to you."

As he spoke, Blue Star was moving toward the several pieces of luggage that rested on the wall rack. In an instant she held a sheaf of paper in her hands, and had settled on the floor in the lamplight. Leaping Bear adjusted the lamp shade to focus light directly on her paper, and she began to read.

With the first line her body began to move to the rhythm of the words. The first poem was a poem of rain, the second of a spring, the third of a river, the fourth of a lake, the fifth of the sea, the sixth of the sky. I listened and felt myself moving with Blue Star—her voice was as liquid as her subject, both a croon and a chant, and her movements were hypnotic.

Leaping Bear had settled in the shadows, and Max was lolling against him. Leaping Bear too was moving to Blue

Star's rhythm, and every now and then his fingers would tap an accent on Max's ribs. Max's eyes were closed in his lolling, but now and again he would open them and look up at Leaping Bear and me and yawn, which in his language said the world was on course, everything was instinctual and right.

When Blue Star finished her reading—her seventh poem, "Of Spirit," was the last—I thanked her. She smiled and nodded and got to her feet to put her poems back in the wallet in the luggage. Then Leaping Bear thanked me, and asked me if I would be staying long at the motel.

"Three days," I said. "We have come to Florida for my nephew's wedding. It's an Easter wedding. We plan to stay three days."

"I wish we could stay three days more." Leaping Bear squatted and laid his hands on Max's head—began massaging the houndish umbrella ears as Max turned his head this way and that. "We must leave tomorrow for Sarasota. We are here to view Karl Wallenda's body and attend his funeral. Karl Wallenda and I worked together in Barnum and Bailey's Circus; you know they have their winter quarters right here in Venice. Blue Star and I thought we would come here first. We have already called Helen and Mario, his son. We used to come here together and we feel close to Karl Wallenda here. Tomorrow we will go to view his body in Sarasota; the funeral is Monday. There will be many circus people there."

"He fell in San Juan, Puerto Rico?" I asked.

"Yes. I wish I had been there, " Leaping Bear said. "Maybe—" he paused. "Sometimes I used to help rig Karl Wallenda's wire. Rigging wire has to be right, especially in a wind."

Blue Star finally spoke. "Maybe Max Father has to go. He has his woman in his car."

"Thank you," I said. "You are both kind beyond my telling." I got to my feet but I could sense that Leaping Bear was not content that Max and I leave.

He was still massaging Max's ears and he suddenly leaned forwards to bury his nose in Max's ears—the left, then the right. He sniffed of each ear several times and then sniffed at each of Max's feet. He looked up at me and smiled with his eyes. "His ears smell like parched corn, have you noticed? His feet smell like the ground."

"Maybe Max Father has to go," Blue Star repeated.

Leaping Bear said: "It is right that you and your woman are here to attend your nephew's wedding, if Blue Star and I are here to attend Karl Wallenda's funeral." Slowly he got to his feet.

Blue Star was nodding. She moved to open the door. Max followed her with his eyes and got to his feet, stretching, yawning, as pleased as could be.

Leaping Bear said: "I never forget the smell of a Black and Tan's ears—or his feet. I grew up with Black and Tans." He moved to block Max's way. "Was his mother—the bitch—was she a large Black and Tan?"

Momentarily I debated—and then decided Leaping Bear would want—deserved—the truth. "His mother was a German shepherd—a registered German shepherd, can you believe it? His father was an unknown."

Blue Star gave Leaping Bear a long look: empathy, reassurance, love.

His face remained inscrutable. He looked down at

Max. "I know his father was a Black and Tan. I grew up with Black and Tans. I didn't have parents or friends, but I had Black and Tans."

He turned to me. "You are a lucky man to own this pup. You are my friend, Max Father." He stepped aside and held out his hand.

I held out my hand. "That's mutual," I said. "Thank you for reading your poetry, Blue Star. Write on! Thank you, Leaping Bear, for being kind to Max and me."

"Be of good spirit," Leaping Bear said. Blue Star nodded. Leaping Bear's hands shaped a shelter above Max's head as we moved into the sunlight.

Worldy Ways

Safely kenneled in our car—his bus—Max attended the Easter wedding and country-home reception for our nephew and his Chris-Evertesque bride. The windows we lowered three or four inches, the bus we moved from the deepest shade of the coconut palms lining the church parking lot to the deepest shade of the orange and lemon trees of the country-home estate, and Max snoozed away the pleasant holiday afternoon.

After dinner Jeanne and Max and I walked down to the Venice Municipal Beach—where Aunt and Uncle and playful pup belong on wedding nights—and Max had his chance to puzzle out his own image in the blue Gulf, to roust out and set flying sea gulls and sandpipers, to stalk and almost catch sand crabs and rock roaches—to do all the things a pup has to do to prove he's an old salt perfectly at home at the seashore. But Max's behavior went beyond such proving—gradually clued Jeanne and me in on fact: he had a new identity.

At first he was a pup playing with the incoming wave, crouching down, mouthing its substance, gnashing his teeth and barking, nipping-while-avoiding its lead fingers; then he was a pup in full chase upon it retreating, but the wave's brother had him and was bearing him out to sea, forcing him to swim for his life. When legs and tail and all his underfur were sloshing wet and cold, they had to be shaken out and dried and warmed by rushing ashore and rolling over in the warm sand, and then the clinging sand itself had to be thrown off like shot from sand blaster—the whole performance a dervish.

Romping and playing pup as the sun disappeared—sank into the sea itself—Max emerged from the waves and stood eyeing Jeanne and me as if to ask what next? Then having twisted his inquisitive head this way and that, he made up his mind, and set off through the white sand to really show what a dog could do in the way of making speed—speed spun in circles that looped round and round the old folks: you traveled so fast you had to lean your body to retain your balance, you had to *cock* a calculating eye—brown gleaming, white showing—just to make sure your parents *saw* how fast you were running, to make sure they kept their eyes on you. So you *cocked* your inner eye, set it shining like a white pearl displayed on the black velvet of your body in all-out speed, as you ran your circles: speed, speed, *speed*—And when your parents began to urge you on, then you ran your doggy legs off in *leaning* circles, leaning circles, leaning circles till your head began to swim and you had to drop to the white sand, your tongue dangling a good four inches of valentine (a word they once used for you) red, vibrating in unison with your heaving black velvet chest. Oh, to be a dog four months of age, and to know who you are and which folks are your folks.! Then you get to your feet and repeat the run—speed, speed,*speed*—on the white sand of Florida, legs slanting, inner eye rolling to your parents' applause—that is what life was meant to be, especially if you had been a pup born into a barrel of straw in the midst of a blizzard in the state of Ohio.

It was clear to Jeanne and me that our Ohio pup had undergone a rite of passage on the Florida beach: it was the young dog of the family making that run. Then he settled in the damp sand as night came on, settled and listened to our exclamations of amazement. And he knew we knew the damp sand was just cool enough to keep you from trying to drink *that water,* which you'd already mouthed and found not to taste right, neither snow nor rain nor mud-puddle right. Yes, pan water will be welcome when we return to our motel: Room #8 not #4, little joke there. Yes, a drink is welcome, thank you. Fill the pan once more, thank you. A guy gets pretty thirsty out there on all that Florida snow that doesn't feel at all like Ohio snow, and cannot be lapped or swallowed. Thank you.

Our second jaunt on the Venice, Florida, beach might have been Max's last, his last on this earth in fact, although neither Jeanne nor I saw it that way as the three of us tripped across the freshly laundered sand the next morning in the rising sun. Ruminating on the wedding and reception Jeanne and I—and Max—traversed the Municipal Beach following the shoreline to the south. Ahead lay the rim of white to match the classic filigree of the new day: no other person or other animal in sight. I stooped and let Max off his leash, and he set off at his doggy lope and that soon had him a hundred feet, then a hundred or so yards ahead of us.

Jeanne and I were plodding, talking quietly. Jeanne was saying how weddings and receptions should be the pattern for all of mankind's doings—they come with their value stamped upon them, hence they are received at something like their true worth—and consequently we know how to celebrate them and be renewed by them.

"Renewed?" I asked. "By a wedding, ha?"

"You were," Jeanne said. "By the dawn's early light in room 8, you were."

"I was?" I laughed. "And ditto to you!"

Caught up in husband-to-wife small talk, what was understood, we sloughed along, concentrating upon the sand, gathering a handful of the night's deposit of new cowries and periwinkles, and the occasional shark's tooth. The shark's teeth especially interested me, for I'd been told they were difficult to find, yet we had come upon a dozen or more in the last few minutes.

At my feet I saw three perfectly serrated grey white teeth the size of small paper clips, and I was stooping to gather them up, when we heard a great shout and commotion just over the sand banks behind us. Suddenly a giant Saint Bernard—surely two hundred pounds of bone and muscle—burst over the sand bank and shot past us. He trailed a six foot length of heavy lead chain and he was being madly pursued by a husky young man shouting "Brut—Brut—stop, stop!"

"Dog on the loose," I remarked to Jeanne.

The lumbering Saint Bernard was throwing sand like a tank, and it was evident the young man was not going to catch him short of his destination.

"He isn't dangerous, is he?" I inquired of the young

man as he came abreast of us and slowed down.

"Not to people, but he's death to other dogs. He's killed five we know of," the young man exclaimed. "He broke this!" He held in his fist the inch thick leather strap of a heavy lead. "I didn't let him loose, I 'm just hired to walk him, and he broke—oh that poor pup, Brutus sees him, is after him. He's a goner!"

He was motioning toward Max who had become aware of the on-charging Saint Bernard and was standing with his umbrella ears raised, his body on point. Max's tail began to wag, but as the on-rushing monster snarled down upon him, he sensed this was not a game. His tail lowered and he turned to run. But where to go? He was cut off from the gulf to his left and hemmed in by the sea-gouged high bank of sand to his rear, and as he glanced toward us it was plain there was no way he could outrun or get past the Saint Bernard.

I was already in all-out sprint and the Saint Bernard's keeper was puffing at my side, but there was no way we could get there in time.

Max did avoid the first leap, but in doing so he had to back further into the cave of the sand bank. The Saint Bernard had stopped and wheeled and was poised to pounce again. This time there was nowhere for Max to go, and the Saint Bernard knew it. Max knew it. And we knew it.

The delinquent keeper by my side was shouting: "Brut, Brut! Stop, stop! Heel, heel!" But we were still yards away, and the frothing Saint Bernard appeared to hear that shout as encouragement to do his damnedest.

He snarled and pranced, pranced and snarled.

Cornered, nowhere to go, Max hesitated—I even imagined he rolled an eye toward me. Then he bared his teeth and dived—straight toward the monster, and disappeared between his front legs.

We were close enough to see but not to help. Then *mirable dictu* Max was standing upright underneath the shaggy body. The Saint Bernard's face registering puzzlement: where the hell had his victim gone?

Puzzlement on that broad brow gave way to pain. Max's needle teeth were taking hold on soft underparts, and the Saint Bernard was whining, trying vainly to get a purchase on Max beneath him, trying vainly to dislodge the teeth whose every gnash racked his giant frame. He could do nothing but howl and collapse and roll on his side, Max hung on and rolled with him. Then the keeper and I were upon the two of them.

The keeper grabbed Brutus' chain and had his full weight wrenching against the choke chain on that mighty neck. I had Max in my hands, my arms. The four of us were entangled, choking, gasping, apologizing.

Then Jeanne arrived and she was calmly asking me, "What was it you were saying before we were so rudely interrupted?"

"Wh—what?" I gasped. At that instant I was blessing Leaping Bear, thanking him for shaping a Cherokee tepee above Max's innocent head.

"You—" Jeanne smiled as she reached out to embrace Max and me, to steady us, "you were holding forth about the educated man being the one who could foresee the furthest reach of any action, and I was about to say *only a god* is endowed with that kind of prescience."

"Leaping Bear—" I began, but I knew Jeanne hadn't seen

and wouldn't know. Instead I said, "Did you see Max? Could you believe what you saw? I want you to swear to it, for it would take a god or goddess' swearing on a stack of bibles—"

"I saw it!" Brutus' sweating keeper exclaimed. He ran a hand through his hair and made a motion as if he wanted to touch Max—make sure he was real—but I waved him off lest Brutus escape again. The keeper went on:"I don't believe it but I saw it." He ducked his head and slid out of the red bandanna neckerchief he wore. He wrapped the neckerchief around his right hand and wound the heavy chain around that fist. "You can say I saw it," he repeated as he turned and drew the chastened Brutus along behind him. "I'll swear it on a stack of bibles."

"Not exactly a deity, but a reliable witness—and larger-than life participant," Jeanne said, motioning after them.

Fast Friends

Max's confrontation with the Saint Bernard on the beach at Venice, Florida, led to his acceptance by Wolfgang Zimmer, the German shepherd of our next door Ohio neighbors. Prior to the Venice trip Max had barely touched noses with Wolfgang, who was three times his size and the acknowledged dominant dog in the neighborhood. Wolfgang was not only the most powerful dog in the neighborhood, but the most famous. After all, for three summers he had ridden up and down Burg Street and its byways in a side-car attached to a roaring, back-firing ancient Harley-Davidson, driven by the goggled aviator-helmeted second son of the Zimmer family.

Wolfgang's motorcycling days were over—Buddy Zimmer had entered the Army as a career officer and was presumably roaring up and down some Autobahn in West Germany in more modern vehicles. But Wolfgang's fame lingered, and had somehow to be communicated to Max. For his part, as the new kid in the neighborhood, Max had been able only to inform Wolfgang that he was going to be gone a few days over Easter.

Now, where our garden met the Zimmer yard, Max stood at Wolfgang's shoulder, doing a little toe-dance, eyes gleaming, notched tongue on display, and announced, "I'm back."

"Where you been, kid?" Wolfgang growled. He lifted his leg to make sure Max didn't forget the corner-pin boundary line separating the two properties. "Come to think of it, I didn't see you around."

"I was down south—way south?" Max said.

"That's like where Burg Street runs into Plum Street?" Wolfgang asked.

"Well, sort of," Max said. He became a bit off-handed in tone: "Kentucky, Tennessee, Georgia, Florida—places like that, you know."

"Can't say as I do," Wolfgang said. "Buddy 'n Me drove the old Harley all around Granville and Granville Township—and I never heard mention of no Kentucky, Tennessee—all that."

"Well," Max said. He leaned down and sniffed the newly anointed corner-pin of the property line just so Wolfgang would know he understood. "You go way down the road—two days driving all day in my dad's bus. As far as you can drive. Then you come to those places—they're states, you know. Ohio's a state, and these are other states."

Wolfgang elevated his head. "Like I told you, Buddy 'n me drove everyplace there is to drive—all around Granville Township, and I never—"

Max nodded, but looked to the horizon. "To get to these places you'd probably have to go in your dad's bus, as far as he could drive in two days. These places are states."

Wolfgang stepped between Max and the horizon, shouldered Max just a trifle. "Buddy 'n me drove everyplace there is to drive in that old Harley. I rode the sidecar, no harness, no straps—just sat in there and rode. I never bothered to ride in my dad's bus."

"I didn't think so," Max began, but added quickly: "You know I've never got to ride in a motorcycle—and a Harley-Davidson at that—wow!"

"So what else is new?" Wolfgang asked. He reached out and wrenched a half-inch limb off a wild cherry sapling, and snapped it into six-inch pieces. "Have you noticed the fox squirrels are coming out of winter quarters, the grays are already out?"

Although the limb-snapping was not lost on him, Max spoke with a traveler's eagerness to be heard: "You see things down south you'll never forget."

"Like what ?" Wolfgang asked.

"You see a white sand beach, like snow only warm, and a Gulf of Mexico."

"What's a gulf—what's that?" Wolfgang asked.

"Well, it's water like Raccoon Creek but not good to drink. It's wider than Raccoon but it doesn't string out—it's just piled up to fill one corner of the sky. It's sort of tied around with white sand that keeps it in place—well, not completely in place, but pretty generally in place."

"Are you sure there is such a thing as a gulf?" Wolfgang asked.

"It's like Raccoon Creek," Max said, "but it's different too. You'd have to see it to believe it."

"I guess I would," Wolfgang said, stretching out his

powerful yellow legs and drawing himself forward so his shoulder muscles rippled. "I guess I'd know how to handle it—"

Max spoke diffidently: "That's another thing—"

"What's another thing?" Wolfgang asked.

"Well," Max shifted his weight to his distant side and spoke softly, "there was a dog down there—he sort of went with the Gulf of Mexico—"

"I said I wasn't really interested in that," Wolfgang said. "What was the dog like?" Wolfgang stretched again.

"Well, he was pretty big—pretty danged big—"

"'Bout my size?" Wolfgang asked. He stretched a third time. "The Labradors down the road—Ben and Bert—they're big. They have to stay in a pen."

"This dog didn't stay in a pen," Max said. "He was being walked and broke his leash. And he was really big—"

"So you said."

"I mean—" Max paused. "He was about the size of you *and* Ben or Bert—but just one dog. Of course he was mixed in color too, sort of brown and white, a mixed-up dog, really."

"Now you are stretching it," Wolfgang said.

"He and I had a little go-around," Max said. He stepped close to Wolfgang. "I came out on the bottom."

"Of course," Wolfgang said. "What'd you expect?"

"Oh, I won the fight," Max said.

Wolfgang snorted. He chuckled. "Now I know you're putting me on. You came out on the bottom and you won the fight, that's a good line!"

"No I'm not," Max said. "I won the fight."

Wolfgang, forgiving a young dog his bragging: "Hey,

let's take a run. If we head over to your dad's walnut woods we can tree a few squirrels—maybe a fox—but a few grays for sure."

"You don't want to hear more about my Florida trip?"

"I'll hear more about it, "I'm sure," Wolfgang said. "But I'll wait till it simmers down to something believable."

Max may not have made a believer out of Wolfgang, but Wolfgang made a gallant out of Max. Or, more accurately, each spurred the other to gallivanting, which comes naturally to a gallant, for when the two of them ran together they sensed they could handle any circumstance—dog or man-made—and dominate any territory from our nearby walnut woods to the distant Gulf of Mexico, the range of their combined travels.

In their many gambols together—like true friends they allowed each other ample private lives—they were intent on proving their capabilities to dogs *and* to human beings. That such noble intentions would lead them and Jeanne and me down most of the side streets of Granville and ultimately to the County Dog Pound in Newark, Ohio, and that such noble intentions would eventually end their friendship tragically, none of us could foresee in April, 1978.

Their first tandem jaunt took them to our walnut woods. They spent the spring afternoon chasing and treeing and generally harassing two families of gray squirrels. Their second run, two days later, took them up the street where they hounded the penned Labradors Ben and Bert by chasing them round and round in their woven wire pen, letting them know that Wolfgang had a new friend Max; their days of combining against Wolfgang had come to an end. Ben and Bert took exception to such a declaration of independence, and only a call from Mrs. Pauling to Jeanne prevented a wire-pulling or worse.

Max and Wolfgang's third run became an escapade. It took place the following Monday afternoon and inticed them a mile down Burg Street to the Denison College campus, where I'm sure Max took a proprietary interest in explaining to Wolfgang: "This is the place where my dad works."

Exactly what stops they made on the Denison campus I don't know, but I found them sacked out in the lobby of the Student Union, along with a dozen students, when I came by at 4:15 p.m. at the end of the day's teaching. Not taking such an infringement on college and state regulations lightly, I got Wolfgang in hand by his chain collar and commanded Max to follow us out the two sets of doors leading from the Union to the quad. All went exactly as it should. Then stern of face and solemn of voice I explained that the Student Union was a place where food was served, and like every restaurant was absolutely off limits, not merely by college decree but by the laws of the sovereign State of Ohio.

Wolfgang was listening with a veteran's disdain for civil niceties, but Max was giving me his complete attention, and I'm sure the lesson was being received in all its profundity, when a beautiful young woman, Polly Edwards, from my class in Contemporary Poetry, chanced by. Polly, her dark eyes like shining beacons, listened to my closing harangue, and then added her own, climaxing it by reading with missionary fervor the eye-high sign posted on the other door: "No Pets Allowed. Unleashed Dogs Will Be Impounded." In lecturing cadence she added: "You'd think administration of this college would put that sign at eye-level for dogs to read, but they're too out-ofsync with life, too *manunkind* to know what it means to deal with living and breathing flesh and blood."

For a moment I took Polly's words literally, and I was about to invoke my dear dead father, his reason, his hold on logic and faith. Then I saw the twinkle in her eyes, her delight in having taken me in. Her tone echoed perfectly my past hour's lecture on E.E. Cummings and his attitude toward the establishment. I had to laugh.

"Polly, you do one pedestrian professor *at this college* to a fine turn."

"To a crisp," she said, smiling, laughing. "But I heard what you said on EEC and society." She turned to Max: "You pay heed to your poppa, Max."

She marched into the Union, and I steered Wolfgang, Max running like a colt at his master's side, off to my car. I got Wolfgang into the backseat and was reaching down urging Max to follow him, when I felt a hand on my arm. I looked up expecting the hand to lead to a Campus Security blue jacket, but it led to a white cashmere sweater belonging to Molly Murphy, a war widow who worked in the Union Snack Bar. She was coming off work, her white costume immaculate, her gray hair and classic face a beautician's advertisement.

"Max is so cute," she exclaimed.

"I hope he wasn't in the Snack Bar." I closed the car door behind Max.

"Oh he was. They both were. That big dog had to be bounced, but Max took his place in line, and when it came his turn he sat down and barked his order. He truly did! I couldn't feed him in the Union—as I explained to him—but I told him to go around to the side door—"

"And no doubt he promptly did?" I asked.

"Three times," she said. "He came back to the line, and then out to the side door. I fed the big one too."

I moaned: "I hope this isn't the beginning—"

"You don't think I did the wrong thing?" Molly Murphy crinkled her eyes. "It was just a bit of hamburger they mooched."

"At least they didn't stay in the Snack Bar," I said. "I found them sleeping in the lobby."

"I told Max to go upstairs to the lobby," Molly said. "And he got the big one to go with him." Again Molly's eyes crinkled.

"You did the right thing, Molly," I said. "By the way, how did you know his name was Max?"

"I got down and read his name-tag." She lowered her voice. "If I had my way we'd allow dogs the run of the campus. Have you noticed how much less turmoil and tension there is on a campus where dogs run loose? Students take out their frustration on dogs, not on other students."

"I agree," I said. "I saw that at Cornell and the University of Maine—even at Harvard one summer."

"And the faculty who want to kick students, kick dogs instead," Molly put in. "Like Dr. Haverford in chemistry and Dr. Wessex in the administration."

"I've seen Haverford at his worst," I said.

Molly Murphy tucked in her cashmere sweater, drew a deep breath and leaned toward me. "Well it all just goes better with dogs doing their thing—even the sex education bit." She waved toward the campus green. "You see a couple dogs doing it and you know it's the fun it's meant to be. And then the damned male looks so hopeless when he's all done but still attached and being led around backwards by his wombus."

"I've noticed that too," I said. I opened the door and got in.

"Male superiority—it's pure piffle," Molly snorted. "And I'm not a damned feminist, not by a long shot."

"You're a damned observant woman, Molly," I said. "You're a gem and a tribute to our Irishry."

"There's your gem; look at that eager face." Molly motioned to Max, who had settled down against Wolfgang but was following our every word. She leaned in the back window and patted Max on his houndish head, and felt his silken ears.

I leaned forward and started the car, but I waited for Molly to return to her Chevy—allowed her quite rightly the privilege of backing out first.

Of course each evening when I picked them up I repeated my professorial do-not-do-it lesson at the outer door of the Union, occasionally pointing in desperation to the eye-height prohibition, but their pattern of behavior was fixed.

Jeanne and I were talking about my dilemma after dinner one evening and Max appeared to be asleep at my feet. I was bemoaning Max's stubbornness, his refusal to learn before he got picked up by the Campus Security, who on a regular basis checked out the Union for dogs, and whose eagle eye he had escaped only by God's grace. I must have sounded as forlorn as a Nantucket foghorn in mid-winter, for Jeanne spoke with spirit: "At least you can be thankful they don't enter Fellows Hall and plague you in your office or classroom."

"Thank God for small favors, as Momma used to say," I remarked. "Why don't they?" Jeanne asked, and I noticed

Max stirred in his sleep, adjusted his legs, twitched an ear.

"Let sleeping dogs—" I motioned and lowered my voice. "It's the revolving door at Fellows Hall. Sectioned as it is, they can't very well cram in with a student, and praise be they don't know how to work a revolving door on their own."

"Have they tried?" Jeanne asked.

"Not that I know of. Oh, Sam Sever in History told me he saw Max waiting beside the downhill side door to Fellows, so he's probably sniffed out where I am, but that downhill door's seldom used, and he can't work the revolving door." No sooner were those words out than Max—had he heard his name?—gave a groan, got to his feet and stretched, and then lay back down on his side facing away from me.

"Maybe you should suggest that the college install revolving doors on the Union," Jeanne continued, "to accommodate Wolfgang Zimmer and Max Bennett."

I raised my finger to my lips. "That'd only cost ten or twenty thou—" I said. "Any other likely suggestions?"

Jeanne thought a moment, then said: "Well, we could always let him have his run in the morning rather than the afternoon."

"Hey, that's a thought?" I said. "The Union's not nearly so used in the early morning—say before mail call at ten or so."

"And without the students to let them in—" Jeanne paused.

"It's worth a try," I said. "That we can do."

The next morning at 9 o'clock I entered the Union through the side door and was pleased to see no sign of Max or Wolfgang, although I had heard them greet one another and set off in a rousing race toward the walnut woods just as I pulled out of our driveway. I lingered a few minutes in the bookstore, off the lobby of the Union, and then sauntered through the lobby and out the doors leading to the campus quad.

I was about to cut across the quadrangle to Fellows Hall when I spotted Wolfgang and Max standing on the broad granite steps of Fellows watching intently the string of students reluctantly making their way to nine-thirty classes. I stopped, and as I watched the last student entered Fellows, the revolving door ceased revolving.

From his vantage point Max walked to the revolving door, inspected it top to bottom, stepped into the first opening, stretched to his full height, hit the door with his front feet, and waited. Nothing happened. He tried the same maneuver a second time. Nothing happened—his weight was not sufficient to swing the door.

"Thank God for small favors," I murmured.

But even as I murmured my gratitude Max turned to Wolfgang and the two of them moved to the door.

Max at his shoulder eyeing him expectantly, Wolfgang stood on his hind feet and laid his weight against the door. His weight swung the door a quarter turn. Now he and Max stood in the small enclosure, half-way home. Again Max waited and Wolfgang stood and heaved his ninety pounds against the door. Voila! Max and he were in the lobby of Fellows. Jauntily exchanging glances, they disappeared down the hallway toward the stairs that led to my office on the fourth floor.

Shaking my head, feeling older and better informed about animals and man, I entered Fellows Hall and climbed the stairs, readying myself for two happy faces that would greet me outside my office door.

Responsibilities

While polishing his Student Union-Fellows Hall act with Wolfgang, Max had undertaken quite another role at West Burg Street. April and May are garden-planting months in central Ohio (May 15 is generally considered to be the frost-free date), and since Jeanne and I have for years raised vegetables and flowers with the zeal and persistence, and sometimes the yields of professional gardeners, we wanted Max to undertake his share of that endeavor. Prior to his coming I had had to give up the growing of melons because of raids by goundhogs and raccoons.

Max took to his chores with alacrity. No matter where he was in the house, any time I entered the furnace room to get into my gardening clothes he would be at my side in a minute, stretching, tail-wagging, speaking his small talk (especially if it was just getting daylight and Jeanne was not stirring), nudging me to stop dawdling and get on with the fun-work. And when we entered the garage where I picked up my gardening gloves and shovel and hoe and whatever other tools were likely to be needed, he bounded ahead and then sashayed down the hill, past the well, doing a quick turn or two to see where exactly I was headed.

His energy never slackened, however laborious the task, however many trips we had to make back up to the garage or house for forgotten tools, for marking line, for seeds. Often such an uphill trip on my part would give rise to a *speed run* on his, circle upon circle with graceful body leaning because of speed, one eye, turned inward, gleaming in its white circle to make sure I beheld his performance.

"This is not the Venice beach! Not the Gulf of Mexico!" I'd shout to him, a shout sure to generate greater speed, for until Jeanne joined us the place where *that run* was perfected was a secret we alone shared.

And when Jeanne did join us, that in itself would bring about a new kind of run—first to the house to escort her through the garage, where she'd often call to me to ask what additional tools she could bring down to save me a trip, and after Max's supervising the selection of the tools, then came a burst of down-hill speed, his arrowing body laid low to the grass and aimed directly at me, at the last instant turning enough to just brush my trousers as he whizzed by.

"Doesn't he ever hit you?" Jeanne asked. "It'd scare me to death."

"Hasn't hit me yet," I replied. "If he does, you'll need a new man. 'Got a new master, get a new man!'"

"You and Caliban!" Jeanne exclaimed. (At Harvard she had accompanied me to Harry Levin's Shakespeare lectures; they were of such quality you wanted your wife to hear them.)

His run finished for the nonce, Max patrolled the strawberry rows, sniffing out rabbit nests, or attended the lifting of a weed pile to locate the field mice. When he found a rabbit or a field mouse or a baby bird he would catch and carry the find on his lips.

Throughout the spring and summer many a baby rabbit, many a weanling mouse, many a nestling robin or ground sparrow, got transported around the yard in what was surely the softest mouth ever attached to a dog. Any number of such finds got returned to their nests—and three weanling rabbits in one morning got transported to the safety of the walnut woods when I was unable to locate the nests from which Max had lifted them.

Later in the summer, when the flowers were in full bloom, the musk- and water-melons just rounding out, the garden in full production, nothing was more pleasant than to sit on the built-up cement foundation of the well, and watch Max doing his regular "row work," patrolling each row up and down in the tomatoes and beans and asparagus—or to watch him moving among Jeanne's Siberian iris, delphiniums, phlox, daisies, day lilies—to see that wagging black flag, its very movement, speed and arc, signifying how close the quarry, how strong the scent. As to the scope of his hunting—well, it had a Maxish freshness always. One moment it was a grasshopper being chased, another moment a butterfly, another a bumblebee or a hummingbird. Often I would turn from getting a drink at the well to discover Max coming proudly toward me, a grasshopper or a cricket, uninjured, on his lip.

One August afternoon I had picked two half-bushel baskets of tomatoes and carried them uphill as far as the well when a neighbor—appropriately named Henry Neighbor—chanced by, ostensibly to check out the tomatoes, obviously to observe and comment on Max. Henry Neighbor complimented me on the tomato crop and said he had meant to speak to me since early spring when he had seen Jeanne or me walking Max on a leash a number of times.

He motioned to where Max was tail-wagging among Jeanne's flowers. "What breed of dog is he?" he asked.

"Well," I explained, "I'm not sure. His mother was a registered German shepherd and his father was an unknown."

"I thought he was a new breed," Henry Neighbor said. "His coat is so sleek and slick—it never seems to pick up burrs or dirt."

"You're very observant," I said.

"No. He joined us the other evening when we had Betsy our cocker on a walk, and later Max came into the house for a drink, and he's neat as a pin. Henrietta rubbed his coat—couldn't get over it. Our Betsy gathers up all the burrs and dirt in the county. She became a walking rat's nest before our eyes, and Max ran right along with her and didn't show a burr, a Spanish needle, a beggar's lice. I told Henrietta I'd drop down sometime and find out what breed he is."

"Here Max—come here," I called.

The wagging tail poised in its motion, the dark head came into view, and Max listened.

"Come here, Max," I called.

He came trotting to the well and stood before us. Henry Neighbor stooped and reached both hands against the sleek back, played his right hand back and forth on the fine black hair, and then looked at his palm.

"I think his body gives off some oil that keeps burrs and dirt from sticking," I repeated.

"Like a danged Scotch-Guarded rug," Henry Neighbor said. "I thought maybe he was a new breed. Henrietta was sure he was."

"I hadn't thought of it that way," I said. "I guess it would be gene-guarded."

"Your wife—did she have a part in it"

"Well," I said, letting the homonym ride, "she really chose him from the litter. There were ten in all; tans, buffs, he was the only black one. His mother was a German shepherd, that much we know. We met an Indian last spring who liked him, and he swore the father had to be a Black and Tan hound."

"I could see how he might think that," Henry said. "But what do Indians know about dogs? Looking at him right now, I'd say if his mother was a German shepherd—" He paused.

"I like to say he has all the alertness of a German shepherd and the sweetness of a hound." I leaned down, cupped my hand, and turned the spigot so Max could get a drink.

"Well." Henry Neighbor took a judge's stance above the lapping Max and emphasized his findings with a finger. "Looking at that feathered tail, and that head, and that body shape—knowing most of the litter was tan or buff—I'd say his father was an Irish setter. Irish setters are my favorite kind of dog, and if Henrietta wasn't the mule she is we'd have got an Irish setter instead of that Cocker Spaniel Betsy that's the pain of my life."

"Sometimes I'm not sure Jeanne and I are equal to owning Max," I put in.

Henry Neighbor inquired quickly: "You don't mean you're likely to get rid of him, sell him?"

"Oh no," I said. "If I sold Max Jeanne would have me

in court for child-selling." Whether responding to my tone or his name, Max yawned and dropped to the hillside and stretched out, exposing his tan underpants to the afternoon sun.

Henry Neighbor smiled, his first smile. "Your Jeanne has something to do with it. I'll tell Henrietta that. That'll get her goat. I'll tell her Jeanne picked Max out of the litter and his mother was a German shepherd and his father was an Irish setter."

Max gave a groan, and a second groan.

I reached down and tugged at his ear. "Your guess is as good as any," I said to Henry Neighbor. "I like the hound notion myself: Max has never had a mean thought in his head."

Max got to his feet and shook himself to rid his coat of bits of newly cut grass that clung to his back. His license and name tags jingled and his ears slapped against his head.

"I'll tell the old woman he's half Irish setter," Henry Neighbor said. He turned and stomped up the hill.

I stooped and grabbed up a double handful of grenade sized tomatoes and caught up with him. "These are for Henrietta—when you tell her."

The Advantage

What Max learned about manners from Molly Murphy at the Student Union, that you take your place in the food line and wait till your turn comes, served him and Jeanne and me in good stead later in the summer. On a broiling afternoon near the end of August Jeanne was canning white peaches—Raritan Roses—but had run out of self-sealing jar lids and granulated sugar so she and Max and I piled into the station wagon to drive to the IGA Store.

"The break from canning will get you away from that hot stove—will do you good," I explained to Jeanne as the three of us drove toward the air-conditioned store.

"It'll be too hot for Max in the car," Jeanne said. "That tarmac parking lot will be boiling and there's not a speck of shade."

"But you saw he wanted to come" I said, asserting the obvious, for Max was always ready to ride in his "bus."

When we got to the IGA, Jeanne and I cranked up the front windows to leave the usual three or four inches of opening. Then we got out and pushed the rear window's air vents to their maximum—the windows of a Le Mans Wagon, ironic name that, don't lower, a feature that earns General Motors a couple dollars extra profit per window, perhaps a couple hundred if it results in the sale of air-conditioning, and inconveniences hundreds of thousands of customers, not to mention Max and all his compatriot back-seat riders. Anyhow, Jeanne and I did what we could by opening the air vents on both sides of Max where he lay panting on his plaid rug, his eyes at half-mast.

"Would we dare leave the front windows clear down?" Jeanne spoke to me across the top of the car in a stage whisper.

I glanced at Max, who appeared drugged by the heat. "Why not," I whispered, "we'll be in the store all of five minutes."

Quickly we rolled down both windows of the driver's seat and hurried into the air-conditioned store. We were inside just long enough to locate and pay for three dozen self-sealing jar lids and two ten-pound bags of granulated sugar—at most ten minutes— but when we returned to the car, Max was gone. I looked around the parking lot; he was nowhere to be seen.

My first thought was that he had leaped out the open window and headed for Raccoon Creek, which ran at its limp summer pace a couple of hundred feet south of the parking lot. The trees lining its bank waited—green and inviting—and I grabbed up his leash and headed in that direction, sounding a come-hither whistle. I was just entering the weedy green beneath the trees when Jeanne called to me, gave me the "yahoo" that I respond to.

She was standing by the car, pointing not to the creek bank but to the north of the parking lot where a sign proclaimed "Harold's Dairy Bar."

"Over there!" she pointed. Sure enough, there was a line of eight or ten children and three or four adults at the order window. Midway in line stood Max. As I watched, two boys at the front got their ice cream and moved aside, and the entire line, Max included, moved up.

"I hope you gave him his allowance, I didn't," I said to Jeanne as I passed the car. She was smiling, laughing, shaking her head to ask "what next?"

When I got to Max he was number three in line, expectantly tilting his head back and forth, awaiting his turn as an elderly man and woman placed their orders. The three children behind him were talking together, but allowing him his place.

"He couldn't have been here long," I said to the round-faced dark-haired girl next to Max as I hooked on his leash.

"About five minutes. He came right ahead of me and Suzy and Earl—"

"Your brother and sister?" I asked, giving my name in return. The three looked as alike as penguins.

"Yes," the dark-haired girl said. "We've been swimming at Lake Hudson and walked over to get a snow-cone. Max got to the line ahead of us and just worked his way along."

"Here Max, you can have seconds on mine," said a red-haired boy who stepped from the shade of a car. He squatted and held the bottom of his cone for Max to bite, then took a bite from the top and held out the remainder of the collapsed cone for Max to finish.

Max crunched down the bits of cone and chocolate ice cream and then licked the sticky hand that held it.

"You know him—you both know him?" I asked in wonderment.

"Hi Bill," the girl said.

"Hi Clara," the boy answered. He was maneuvering his hand to expose his wrist so that Max could get at a chocolate stain.

"Oh yes," the girl named Clara said. ""We ride Bus #5 and are in Mrs. Hennesey's seventh grade class. Everybody in our class knows Max."

"He and that big German shepherd met our bus as we unloaded at school for a week or so this spring." Bill said. "They came back at recess one day too."

Clara pushed Suzy and Earl ahead to the order window, and added: "We all got to play with them at recess. You can do sticks or tag or anything with Max—anything—but the shepherd's different."

"He growls if you bump him," Bill explained.

"Or take hold of a stick he wants." As Clara spoke the memory of her voice came back to me. I asked her:"Are you the Clara Wunsch who called and told me Max was down at the school, and the teacher was going to call the police?"

Clara placed her own order for a cherry snow-cone. "I'm the one," she said, smiling at Bill. "Max stood in line there too, right where we queue up to file into the school. He lined up and barked to be let in, but Mrs. Hennesey wouldn't let him."

"So he kept barking," Bill added.

"That's when Mrs. Hennesey said she was going to have to call the police and I went to the phone and called the number on Max's tag."

"That was very nice of you," I said. "I really appreciate your calling me. Look," I said, including Bill in my offer, "would you all care to have something else—or let that snow-cone be on Max?"

"Oh no," Clara said. "Thank you very much. We have a regular allowance—we really do." She had unsnapped a red coin purse and was paying for the three snow-cones.

"I wish you'd let Max treat you."

"He already did. He played with us at recess." Clara said. "And when he got tired and lay down he folded his feet one over the other, like hands, like he was saying thank you or crossing himself."

"He's really neat," Bill said. "I'll bet if our class could have a dog he'd be the one we'd choose."

With that compliment ringing in our ears Max and I turned and headed back to Jeanne. She had thoughtfully opened all four doors and the car waited like a mother hen with her wings spread waiting for her straying chicks.

Naturally I assumed the debt we owed Clara, and Suzy and Earl Wunsch and the red-haired Bill had to go into God's Account Book of Kindnesses Unrewarded, but I hadn't reckoned with Max. Just how much he understood of every conversation I can't say, but I do know he took off like a shot right after breakfast the third day following our encounter at Harold's Dairy Bar. Within half an hour our phone rang and I recognized the voice of Clara Wunsch.

"I thought I should tell you Max is here at our house on Summit Street," she said.

"It's so nice of you to call—this second time," I said. "What's your number? I'll be right down to get him,"

"Well, our number is 13 Summit but—"

I could sense I had spoken too soon, had presumed.

She went on: "Would you mind if we just kept Max till

noon? I've promised Suzy and Earl we'd play with him."

"Oh, that's fine—that's quite all right." I said.

"I think he wants to play with us. He's playing stick with Earl and Suzy—they're throwing it off the porch and he's going for it right now," Clara said.

"Wonderful!" I said. "Suppose I come there to your house at lunch time. Would right at twelve—"

"Well—"

Again I could sense Clara Wunsch and Max were tuned to a wave length I knew nothing about. Clara's voice came with some feeling for nuance. "If you wouldn't mind terribly, we'd like to meet you down at Fuller's Market. We'll take Max there and get him a bone after we play with him. I've already called Bill Hiller—you met him at Harold's—and he's going to come over awhile and then go with us. I've already promised Max we'd do that."

"Wonderful!" I said. "I'll see you all there at Fuller's, there by the drinking fountain, at twelve. Would that be about right?"

"Just right," Clara Wunsch said softly. "Bill and I and Suzy and Earl and Max will see you then."

She hung up and I went down to the flower garden to explain to Jeanne Max's whereabouts.

Jeanne stood in the morning sun where it found its earthly complement in phlox and marigolds, where bumblebees in black and gold colors rode blue and purple delphinium spikes around breezy tracks scented by artemisia and day lilies. Somehow the something I couldn't express, was, and would always be, as long as Max and Clara and Jeanne and their kind existed.

Testing the Boundaries

At high noon that sunny day I stood on the broad sidewalk in front of Fuller's Market, under the green awning announcing "Baskets from all over the world." Before me a tableau: Max encircled close up by four admirers, and at a slightly greater distance, by curious shoppers as he eagerly awaited trimmed-out T-bone steak bones offered by Earl and Suzy Wunsch, both of them kneeling in front of their tail-wagging, bone-cruncher at eye-height. The younger Wunsches were as observant as their older sister. Earl exclaimed over the gleaming teeth, the red-notched tongue, while Suzy commented on the way the muscles in Max's dome-shaped head moved as he worked his powerful jaws, jaws that I've read were capable of exerting over seven hundred pounds of pressure per square inch. And when a particle of bone fell to the sidewalk, Earl or Suzy retrieved it and held it to be sniffed by Max and then seized, deftly, ever so careful of the small fingers that held it.

At twelve midnight of that same day I was speeding toward the Granville Municipal Garage, under the Columbus Road viaduct, in response to a telephone call from the Granville Police dispatcher who informed me the patrolman had picked up two rampaging dangerous dogs, one a black and tan identifiable by his name tag and telephone number, hence the call, and the other a large German shepherd. When I arrived in the muddy, foul-smelling nether regions under the viaduct, surely the purgatory if not the hell of fair Granville, I found Max and Wolfgang each tied with a length of worn inch-thick hemp to a detached snowplow, both raising the roof with their protests.

The patrolman, whose purring cruiser's headlights cast giant animal shadows on the surrounding wall, informed me: "These two marauders were found roaming the lower campus, a definite threat to life and limb, to persons and property."

"You yourself picked them up?" I inquired.

He ignored my question and felt in the cruiser seat for a notebook and ballpoint pen. "Do you admit ownership of either of the animals in question?"

I went over to Max, who had changed his howling protests to yips of "Thank-god-I-see-my-poppa." Wolfgang too stopped his deep-lunged protests and began giving forth the low whimpering that caused Mrs. Zimmer to characterize him "the biggest ham actor outside T.V. soap opera."

"This one—Max—is ours." I said. "The German shepherd belongs to our next-door neighbors, the Zimmers. Could they both be released to me?"

"You admit to ownership of one of the dogs in question?" the patrolman went on. "You have some identification?"

"Would you believe me if I were to deny ownership?" I asked. Max's head and neck had canted at an angle against the heavy rope causing him to wheeze with every breath as he sought to touch my hand. I took out my wallet and held out my driver's license. "If you could release both dogs to me I'll see that—"

"Not so fast, not so fast," the patrolman said. "Just give me—is this your present address?" He was matching my bearded face to the one on the license, finding enough similarity to begin writing. "Are you employed?"

"I teach at Denison," I said.

"Well, then, you know the law is the law, and Granville Village ordinance requires every dog to be secured—the operative word is *secured*—at all times day and night. Is this address—West Burg Street—is that in the village or the township?"

"Township," I said. "It's pretty difficult to keep a dog secured day and night. We have a large garden—"

"Are you the Denison prof who brings the vegetables to Fuller's Market?"

"I'm that guy," I said. I reached down and untied the heavy rope restraining Max and slowly worked it through his collar. He leaped and gave me a kiss and then stood looking from me to his "bus" as if saying "let's get the hell out of here." Then he went over to Wolfgang and nosed at him, at the rope on his neck.

"When you raise a garden," I said, "you almost need a dog, a dog with some room to maneuver, to control groundhogs and raccoons, even rabbits."

"I raise a garden myself," the patrolman said. "I know

what you mean." He looked at Max and then at the whimpering Wolfgang. "But the law is the law and I mean to enforce it."

"So I understand," I said. "You've done the right thing, the necessary thing—and I'll be glad to go to mayor's court to pay the fine."

"There'll be no fine this time, since you came right down," the patrolman said. He pointed at Max and motioned toward the car.

"I'd like to take—rid you of both dogs," I said. "I'll see that Max is kept closer home, and I'll tell the Zimmers they should do the same with Wolfgang."

"You do that," the patrolman said. "By the way, your hound got into the cruiser on his own when I told him to."

"He likes to ride," I said. I was untying the rope that held Wolfgang who was straining toward Max.

"You might want to keep an eye on your hound; he'd be easy to steal," the patrolman said

"Thank you," I said. "I've thought about that."

"It'd be a shame to lose a dog like him." The patrolman reached toward Max—then changed his mind—and pointed.

"You're so right," I said.

"I don't think I could have caught that German shepherd if your hound hadn't got in the cruiser when I told him to. Once your hound was in, the other decided he'd go along."

"They're really great pals," I said. "You'd hardly believe this but sometimes when they're together and I call Max, Wolfgang will actually grab Max and hold him by his head, even bowl him over and pin his head to the ground, to keep him from coming to me." As I spoke I had opened the door to the station wagon and Max had climbed in, followed by

Wolfgang.

"They appear to be pals," the patrolman observed.

I closed the door on Max and Wolfgang, and held out my hand.

The patrolman began to reach for my hand but again, thought better of it. He motioned toward the two faces that hung expectantly over the front seat, ready for their driver. "You understand you've had your warning. The next time it's the Dog Pound, and that means a fine or worse."

"I understand," I said. I leaned forward and started the motor. "The question is do Max and Wolfgang?"

"They better."

Problems at Hand

Keeping Max secure was easier to promise than to do, especially when fall came and Denison classes began, but Jeanne and I made an honest effort. We bought a double-length chain to "secure" him to the maple tree on the patio behind the house when we were working in that area or sitting at the picnic table, and we bought a "1000-pound test" nylon rope to which we attached a "sure-grip" snap fastener to anchor him to a concrete block when we were working in or near the garage. Then too, Jeanne took him on regular morning walks—on leash, and I took him on late afternoon or evening strolls—on leash—when I came home from classes or evening meetings.

Just how much traveling he had done and how many friends he had made in the student body and jogging fraternity we began to understand when the college joggers—students and faculty—once again began running on Burg Street. Since our trip to Florida when as a young pup he had followed the legs of the men delivering bread at the IGA Store in New Albany, he had shown a proclivity to match legs in motion, an obsession to run with all runners. Now, as the joggers—young and old, men and women—passed at the end of our drive, it was a twenty-four-hour undertaking to keep Max "secure," to keep him from getting free to set his own legs in motion.

And the times he did manage to get off his chain or nylon rope and out of the house without being "secure," we could count on finding him with a set of joggers, oftentimes accompanying them to their dormitories or at least as far as the Denison Field House, where they showered and dressed. His range of those who knew him was legend.

One evening at dusk, with a leash in hand, I had given Max momentary freedom from the nylon rope to accompany me to our mailbox. His eye being keener than mine, he caught sight of a jogger just coming over the hill, headed our way. Ignoring my command he dashed down the road a good quarter mile, joined the solitary jogger and accompanied him stride for stride. On they came, up the road past the mailbox, where the jogger, a student I had never met, held his motion running in place until I had Max secured on his leash.

"Thanks very much," I said to the student.

"That's okay," he said. Still jogging in place he quietly added: "See your later, Max," then let out his legs and took off in his graceful stride that ate up the macadam of Burg Street. How and under what circumstances he had come to know Max I never was able to determine.

Or the night Max worked the snap off the nylon rope and disappeared taking the snap with him. I discovered him gone right after dinner and immediately drove to the College Union, thinking I'd find him there and "bus" him home. But he was not at the Union, nor at the Field House, where half a dozen or so students responded to my whistle by asking: "Are you looking for Max?"

I *was* looking for Max, but he was nowhere to be found. Disconsolate, I returned home, and Jeanne and I spent the evening waiting for a phone call that did not come. The next morning I was just finishing shaving—one does shave a bit to keep a beard in trim—when Jeanne called to me. "You're wanted on the phone."

"Could you take it?" I said.

"They want to speak to Mr. Bennett," Jeanne said.

"Police—Dog Pound?" I asked as I moved toward the phone.

"Mr. Bennett—" began a familiar, warm voice.

"Polly Edwards—how *are* you? I've missed you in Modern Poetry this term," I said.

"I miss you too," she replied. "But I've got your dog."

"Max?" I exclaimed. "You've got him?"

"He's here with me in Shaw Hall. He's been here all night. I had phone duty and it was so cold that when he showed up about ten p.m. I just got him to stay. He sat close to me all night long and kept me warm. I knew you wouldn't mind."

"I don't mind, not at all," I said. "The lucky dog! My golly, I feared—I just asked Jeanne if your phone call was the Granville police or the Licking County Dog Pound."

"You do sound sort of relieved," Polly Edwards said.

"Am I ever!"

"You know I made Max make me a promise *you'll* have to keep."

"He made *you* a promise *I'll* have to keep?"

"Yep. If he ever has puppies—sires a litter, you know, does his part, I get one. He promised me that!"

"I promise that," I said. "I'm marking that beside Polly Edwards in my memory. You can count on that." I paused. "And I'll be right up to get Max; he missed his supper and I'll be he's plenty ready for breakfast."

"He already had breakfast. My roommate brought us each a sweet roll and Max just finished his—and two pint cartons of milk." Polly Edwards paused and then added: "As EEC would say, I'm not exactly man-unkind."

"Cummings would love you, I know Max does." I added: "I'll be at Shaw within ten minutes."

"Take your time," Polly said. "Max'll be right here like the honey he is."

During the fall and winter when Jeanne walked Max daily, Wolfgang went along. Neighbors became accustomed to seeing the three of them, Jeanne with Max on leash—"attached to his mother by a cord," as we phrased it—being escorted by the giant German shepherd. Wolfgang usually tramped ahead as a lead-dog might, but sometimes he ran to the side taking a schoolboy's delight in breaking the film ice in the ditch with his huge paws, and his powerful yellow legs. Splashing through the smelly ditch water Wolfgang became every inch the outdoor animal he was: year-round he slept out of doors, and over winter his coat became a shaggy beast-of-the-deep-wood mat. Only his voice with those dear to him betrayed Wolfgang as the whimperer and grumbler, the lovable warm-hearted boob the Zimmers and Jeanne and I knew him to be.

By some strange transference of his attachment to Max, Wolfgang became quite possessive of Jeanne. He would do whatever she asked him to do, except *not* follow her. Thus it came about one wintry Friday morning that while Max was safely kenneled in our sunny living room, no doubt curled into a dreamy ball on his own covered couch, Jeanne began walking the mile-and-a-half to downtown Granville to keep a dental appointment. As she strode briskly along she became aware that Wolfgang had heard her and had begun following at a distance of several hundred feet. Half a dozen times she stopped and begged, and finally commanded, him to go home, but he persisted.

As Jeanne recounted the experience, she made it to Dr. Leon Sturgeon's dental office on the ground level of the old Opera House just in time for her appointment, and she was promptly ushered into the inner office and seated in the dental chair by Mrs. Smith, the nurse and an old family friend. No sooner was Jeanne seated than she and Mrs. Smith and Dr. Sturgeon became aware there was a great thumping on the outside door. Mrs. Smith rushed out, only to return a moment later, white-faced and shaken, to declare to Dr. Sturgeon that a mammoth dog was standing up lunging at the door, threatening to break it down.

"That would be Wolfgang," Jeanne explained to Dr. Sturgeon.

"Your dog?" Dr. Sturgeon asked.

"Our neighbor's dog, a friend of our Max," Jeanne replied. "He goes with us on all our walks."

The outer door continued to rattle and shake in its frame, accompanied now by a deep braying.

"What do we do?" Mrs. Smith exclaimed. "He'll break the door down."

"He's used to working the revolving door at Fellows Hall," Jeanne said. "I'll go and try to explain it to him, if you like. I tried to get him *not* to follow me, but he *would* come along."

"What do we do?" Mrs. Smith moaned, as the thunderous noise continued.

"You could just let him in," Dr. Sturgeon said, laughing. He himself went to the outside door and opened it.

Wolfgang bounded into the reception room, then followed his nose to the inner office, where he nudged Jeanne and, whimpering with joy, settled his huge frame into the space between the wall and dental machine and began licking and cleaning his paws.

That was Jeanne's account of Wolfgang's arrival at the dental office, the remainder of the account I overhead as Wolfgang told it to Max the next morning, standing in their favorite trysting spot where our garden abuts the Zimmer yard.

"I think there must be something wrong with your mother." Wolfgang said. "She had a bad time yesterday."

"Like having a toothache?" Max said. "Needing a filling?"

"Like not having a good mechanic," Wolfgang growled, "and not having good drinking water. She wanted to ride in a sidecar but they didn't ever get the motorcycle started."

"She went to the dentist," Max said.

"That mechanic in the white coat," Wolfgang grumbled. "He don't even know his tools. He has to have some woman hand them to him."

"Dr. Sturgeon. He's a doctor of dental surgery, and a darned good one," Max said. "That woman in white is Mrs. Smith, she's a registered nurse."

"They don't know how to grind a thing. They've got a

grinder that works by foot pressure but they don't know the first thing about grinding a valve. When Buddy 'n Me was driving the old Harley-Davidson we overhauled the engine twice and did a valve job both times, and we didn't even have a grinder that works with foot pressure—"

"Dr. Sturgeon was grinding my mother's tooth, for Pete's sake."

"Look Max, I was there and I saw the whole thing from beginning to end."

"Then you saw my mother getting a tooth filled by Dr. Sturgeon."

"I know what he was doing," Wolfgang said. "They had your mother fastened in this sidecar, and they put a bib on her, and gave her a drink of water but it wasn't good and she had to spit it out."

"I think that's part of filling a tooth," Max said. "I didn't get to see it but I heard my father and my mother—"

"I was here, and I did see it," Wolfgang said. "This mechanic in the white coat said, 'I'll grind it down a little more. Try that.' He never did get the valve right because the motor never started."

"I heard my father—" Max began but Wolfgang nudged him to silence.

"He'd run his grinder and your mother'd get thirsty with all that waiting, and he's say, 'Drink this. Spit that out. Drink this. Spit that out.' Then he'd grind some more. Then he'd ask the woman mechanic for another tool. He just don't know how to grind a valve—and something more."

"What more?"

"He never did get the trip started. Finally he asked your

mother to step down and then he said, 'That'll be twenty dollars,' and all the ride your mother got was up and down, and it wasn't worth it."

"I think all that goes with getting a tooth filled," Max said.

"I was there and saw the whole thing," Wolfgang said.

"I don't think you saw it clearly. I think you may have a bad feeling—against a doctor of dental surgery."

"I don't have a bad feeling against anybody," Wolfgang said. "How could I have a bad feeling against that head mechanic, the one in the white coat? He may not know his tools but he's the one that let me in the door, and he said something very nice about me."

"Like what?"

"When he was grinding the valve and trying to get it smooth but not doing it, he stopped and said, 'It's getting hot in here and Wolfgang smells like a barnyard.'"

"He said that about you?" Max asked in wonderment.

Wolfgang drew himself up at the shoulders and shook out his coat from ears to tail. "Sure he did. He said I smelled like a barnyard. You just ask your mother if he didn't say that. And what's more, she agreed. She said, 'He does indeed.'"

"Well," Max said, "that is a nice compliment. That really is. I'd like to have someone say that about me."

Celebrity

As Max was drawn to joggers, so he was drawn to crowds. He was a natural for Denison's early fall and late spring classes on the lawn, for field trips, fraternity and sorority parties, athletic events, lectures—almost any collection of people where there would be excitement and good times—food, drink, voices, action. And he had an uncanny gift for sniffing out such occasions, for adjusting his behavior to the occasion, to fit in, to make things go in good spirit. His "audiences" through the years are too numerous to detail, but they ran from an outdoor reception for Denison Trustees and Faculty during Homecoming Weekend (which he attended with Wolfgang until Jeanne and I got the two of them in hand and safely to the car), to parties in many private homes in Granville.

To cite but a few of the latter: the Sanchez family had been entertaining out-of-town guests from Columbus *and Max*. They called. He had been with them for the afternoon, and he would be brought to my car by the daughters if I'd just drive slowly up Maple Street, off Pearl, till I saw two dark-haired girls, ages eight and ten, with Max on a leash. I did, they were, he was.

Then there was the call from the Fieldcrests, one of the patriarchal founding families of the town. They had held their annual family reunion on Prospect Street, where, the caller said, Max had been in attendance. When I arrived to pick him up, I found him tied by a length of new clothes line to a wire run. He had been supplied a bowl of roast chicken and dressing and a second bowl of ice water with cubes in it.

To prove that he was as open to science as to the humanities and the arts, Max attended several lectures in Herrick Hall, the chemistry lecture hall. And I received a call one afternoon from the distinguished research scientist, Dr. Hans Burford and his wife. They had Max with them and he would be found sitting with them on their front porch on Elm Street—as he was.

Then there was a call from Chalmers Morrison on Sunrise Street. Max had struck up an acquaintance with him as he was enroute to the golf course to pick up his wife. Max had not only gone to the golf course, but he had taken an afternoon swim in the pond, and he had accompanied the Morrisons back to their house. I drove Max's "bus" into the Morrison drive, secured Max, and started to back down, only to have Mr. Morrison dash out to the car to tell me: "By the way, we fed Max before calling you. Mrs. Morrison thought you ought to know in case he slights his supper."

And there was the woman painter on Welsh Hills Road, who said, "I've got your dog Max chained here in my backyard. I saw him up the street and I could see at a glance he is far too valuable a dog to be let loose, so I went after him." When I arrived on Welsh Hills Road, the woman-artist questioned me closely on Max's parents, his breeding, and objected strongly to my use of the term "Black and Tan."

"I much prefer 'coal and walnut' to describe him. Please use these terms, these colors. And those eyes of his—look at them closely, they're chestnut. Now you be sure to use those colors to describe him"

Unusual, yes. But Max brought out the creative—for good or ill—in everyone. And I'd like to think, because of the tragedy in the offing, that he brought out the good in Eleanora Angelico. Eleanora was one of those statuesque Hellenic beauties such as Edgar Allan Poe wrote about. After all, Eleanora is a version of "Helen." and looking at her you could barely keep from saying:

Helen, thy beauty is to me
Like those Nicean barks of yore
That gently, o'er a perfumed sea,
The weary, way-worn wanderer bore
To his own native shore.

Although I did not know Eleanora Angelico well, I knew her on a first name basis, and she called while I was listening to the late news at eleven o'clock on a Wednesday night.

"Are you the owner of a dog named Max?" she began. "He has this number on his name tag."

"Eleanora," I said, "this is Max's father. Is Max down there at the Inn?"

She was laughing. "He walked in just a short while ago with two businessmen from Cleveland. I tried to explain to him that we had a reservation for them, and we didn't have a reservation for him. He sat there taking in everything I said, twisting his head from side to side, as if to say, 'That's odd. I am sure one was made in my name.' Now he's outside barking."

"Oh my god, Eleanora," I exclaimed. "I'll be right down. Tell him his bus is coming."

When I drew up at the Inn I found Eleanora and two young women with Max at the porte-cochere. I recognized the women as waitresses. I offered my apologies and added: "I hope he didn't really cause a problem."

"He couldn't cause a problem," Eleanora said, laughing. "He's more fun than two businessmen from Cleveland could be, even if they had reservations and he didn't."

"We went off work a while ago and hung around to visit with Max," one of the waitresses said.

"We fed him a couple servings of walnut cake," said the other. "We hoped that would be all right."

"You spoil him and me," I said, understating the obvious.

Eleanora had stooped and said goodbye to Max and I had got him into the car; "Just a sec—"she called. Graceful in high heels and long gown, a goddess in the moonlight, she stepped to the car, leaned in the back window, and spoke quietly to Max.

He listened with his usual complete attentiveness and then slowly reached up and touched noses with her, a goodbye rite he takes very seriously.

To this day I have pondered that half-light farewell, for the next time I saw Eleanora Angelico she was lying on her funeral bier, victim of a car crash.

A Mutual Pact

When Jeanne and I acquired Max she had said that we had much to learn from him, and I had asserted that he had much to learn from us. This difference of opinion probably tells more about Jeanne and me and our upbringing and openness, or lack thereof, than a reader cares to know. But in retrospect I am happy to confess that Jeanne was right and I was wrong. And Max made learning so easy that even I could pass his course. That course was the study of joy, and Max found ways to convey joy that would leave a wordsmith wordless.

Asleep or awake, he took joy in giving pleasure. Even in preparing to sleep he found a way to be Max the playful, Max the hound. Most dogs lower themselves to the ground or floor with muscles as taut as piano wires; Max simply turned his muscles limp and "dropped," like a bag of bones falling. Often Jeanne and I would be in another room or on another floor of the house and we would hear Max's body "crash" and look to one another and smile—

And then we would enter the room and find him asleep, not on his stomach but on his back, his "walnut" underbody, his front legs in the air, sometimes stiff-leggedly so, sometimes folded at the wrists, his back legs lolling open, leaving his private parts and himself as vulnerable as an animal can be—how could one not learn openness and trust from such teaching?

And as he slept we would see the legs tense and begin to move, obviously running, the run become a dash, the dash a pounce—oh, butterflies, grasshoppers, moles and field mice stay alert: Max in his dreams is at large, among you, upon you, beyond you Or—a few minutes later—to hear the mouth begin to work, and to realize he had come back from a hard chase—still sound asleep—and was at his waterpan or feed bowl being replenished. Other times, a more infantile Max would begin to whimper, disturbed, disconsolate. Or begin to suck, and you sensed he was back with his regal mother, back with his sisters and brothers, worming his way among those warm furry bodies to her warm full dugs.

Or, when the legs remained still in soundest sleep, the tail would begin to wag, to thump the floor. Sometimes when he was on his couch, sound asleep, the tail would shake free, fall over the edge of the couch and begin to sway like a beautiful pendulum telling joy: sweet dreams, life's pleasantries made manifest.

Jeanne and I, beholding Max asleep, could not help but find our world clocked to joy and trust and love. We named Max's sleeping on his back, his "walnuting," in part to record the beautiful color of the sun's catching the fine hairs of his underbody, in part to acknowledge the vulnerability of his private parts.

Awake, Max was capable of teaching while standing still. I see him holding a point in various postures, on four legs or three, with head and ears cocked, even his eyes locked and gleaming. And in that fixed stance he was likely to be stalking a snake, a chipmunk, a squirrel, a rabbit, a groundhog. Or, if looking skyward he seemed to have telescopic vision to spot each crow, hawk, buzzard, plane, or helicopter.

But it was when awake and in motion that Max proved his houndish best, not merely in performing his circular *speed* run but when chasing a rabbit flat-out, or flat-out responding to his own special whistle that could bring him from beyond our sight—to make a joyful leaping arrival that placed a kiss on Jeanne's or my cheek: "Here I am, joy to you!"

By such exemplified teaching Jeanne and I became "Maxish" in our thinking: able to sense what was going on in that domed head and take pleasure in that cognizance. Impossible, you say. Well, not impossible but challenging and difficult. Let me cite an instance.

In walking on campus between the parking area and Fellows Hall I noticed Max eyeing a certain college wall, broken to the side with a set of steps. His fascination was with the wall; anyone could walk the steps; and his thought, strong as if he had shouted it was this: I am considering that more direct route, but I do have some doubts about that leap.

Several times in going back to the car when I let him off the leash I saw him go to the wall like a world-class high jumper gauging the bar, getting his distance, psyching himself, as Dwight Stone might say, "working out the mechanics of his jump." But he didn't jump, not the first, nor the second, nor the third time.

Then there came the day when he was ready, and he hung back and waited while I went down the steps and around, so the wall was between us, and then he set off and gathered his body and leaped—not merely to clear the wall, which would have made it a spectacular jump, but to clear the wall *and* the yews growing beyond it—making it a high and a broad jump, *a true Max leap!* Done for the zest, the fun!

And after the leap, the rush to me for that word of praise which was his Olympic medal and star-spangled song combined.

Max had prepared me for his leap—so that I might share it and take pride in it—time and again he surprised Jeanne and me, intentionally surprised us with subtlety of thought and act. On such occasions Jeanne and I could but shake our heads and ask one another, how does he think things through with such clarity, such insight?

But one instance: the mid-February night he came from home to campus to wait for me after I had driven off to a meeting while he was eating his supper.

Snow covered the ground—several inches deep—and he had to wait for me to come to the car. And he did wait. But he did not lie beside the car (he often waited beside the car during summer runs to campus) but in this freezing mid-February night he waited *on the car.*

I found him curled up on the radiator drawing its warmth from underneath, his nose buried deep in his feathery tail. And when I came to the car, he stood up and stretched and then leaped down in his boneless ease and nudged my hand and got inside the car for the ride home, the casualness of his every movement saying, "Sure, any hound would know to wait on the warm radiator."

Enemy Alert

In early spring of Max's third year of life I took up jogging as a substitute for rope-jumping, the exercise I had practiced since childhood. In part I suppose I took up jogging because it was modish, but mainly I took it up because it permitted Max to join me. Had I foreseen the consequences of my jogging with Max running by my side I'd have stuck to swinging the rope and left jogging to be exploited by the masterful Jim Fix and others.

Lest you leap to a wrong conclusion, let me quickly say that it was not a passing car that brought our jogging to a dire end. No, it was our well-intentioned neighbor Henry Neighbor, who chanced to be out walking his Cocker Betsy, accompanied by his forty-two year old brother Randolph, a Marine sergeant who was visiting with him.

I had never met Randolph Neighbor but I knew him by word-of-mouth. He had been—Henry told me—a star athlete in high school, one with professional possibilities in football, basketball, and baseball, a triple-threat athlete of whom it could truly be said: "When the going gets tough, the tough get going."

Henry's description of his brother had been sufficiently vivid and complete that when Max and I passed them and the Cocker Betsy going out the road I merely raised my hand and waved. But Henry *would* have me meet his brother and so on our return run he stepped into the road and held up his hand.

Although I knew Jeanne had set out for town and I was running a trifle late to allow time for bathing and breakfast, I stopped and unsnapped Max from his leash, thinking he could have a moment's romp with Betsy—they were good friends—while I did the obligatory handshaking.

"I was telling Randy about your Max," Henry Neighbor began once the introduction was made.

"He says he's some dog," Randy exclaimed. He looked toward Max who had bounced toward Betsy and picked up a stick, inviting a game of chase.

"He's too frisky for his own good at the moment," I said as Max tossed the stick in the air, caught it, dropped it, caught it up and whipped his body around an oak tree, paused there, half-concealed, inviting Betsy to try to grab the stick.

"You'll have to feel Max's fur; it's as sleek as a mink," Henry said to his brother. To me he added, "Give Max a whistle—"

"I was about to go," I explained. "I'm running a little late and have to make a nine-thirty class."

"Give Max a call," Henry said. "Here Max! I want you to meet my brother."

I could see there was no putting Henry off, so I whistled twice, and Max whirled from Betsy and dashed toward us, gave me a kiss on the cheek as he went by and came to a stop, a crouch, ten feet away.

"Max," I announced, "this man wants to meet you. This is Randy Neighbor, Henry's younger brother. He's an athlete *and* a Marine."

My tone or hand movement must have been excessive, for Max took a couple steps and leaped up to plant a kiss on Randy Neighbor's cheek.

"Max old boy!" Randy Neighbor exclaimed.

Accepting the welcome Max again leaped up to kiss a cheek, and as he did so Randy Neighbor whirled his body and swung his knee with as much power as he must have used when he was establishing himself as a likely professional in football.

His knee crunched—resounded—against the point of Max's chest, and the blow lifted Max high, turned him completely over in the air.

"You should teach your dog never to leap on people," Randy Neighbor announced. He said several other things which I didn't quite hear, for I was kneeling, trying to take Max in my arms, where he lay gasping for breath, gagging on his tongue, saliva and blood filling his mouth.

As I worked over Max I became aware that two sets of legs momentarily stood beside us, that for an instant a Cocker face peered at us, and then I was alone with Max, getting him into my arms, carrying him to the station wagon, trying to open the door and get him onto his side on his plaid cover without further damaging his chest.

I know I had to go into the house for the car keys but I wasn't aware of doing that. I was too busy explaining to Max that he would be all right, that he had just met a manunkind, that Dr. Sanders in Alexandria would make him well again.

Dr. William Sanders, long-time friend and superb student of the arts and veterinarian medicine, held the door as I carried Max into his office. We did not lift Max to the examination table but stood him on his feet beside it. There he wobbled and trembled and leaned against me while Dr. Sanders laid the stethoscope here and there on his chest. Then I talked to Max and held his mouth and Dr. Sanders swabbed at the blood, peered into his throat. Reassured by word and hand Max resettled himself on his feet and began to breathe with greater ease, with some regularity.

"Had you not told me,' Dr. Sanders was saying, talking fast as was his habit, "I would have assumed he'd been hit by a car. How any man, any human being, could do this to any dog and especially to you, Max—" He began gently fingering Max's chest, exploring the bruised and swollen point where the powerful knee had done its worst. He straightened and said:

"The ribs are probably cracked, but they haven't splintered, haven't pierced a lung or he'd be coughing blood or bleeding internally. Dogs are remarkably strong, remarkably recuperative. And the toughest of all are these good old hounds." His voice became a croon: "You've got some good genes in that battered frame, Max. Yes you have. Yes you have. You've got some damned good genes in that old hound frame." He leaned to an ear. "Hear that, Maxie?"

"That blood in his mouth?" I asked.

"From the tongue. He ran a tooth into that already-notched tongue. No problem there. It has practically stopped bleeding. No problem at all." Again Dr. Sanders knelt to be at Max's chest level and again he inspected that chest wound, fingering it ever so lightly. The merest touch caused Max to wince and whimper, to fix his eyes on my face: "Why?"

"Max," I said, unable to answer for our kind.

"Max," Dr. Sanders said, "you're going to be okay. You don't think so at the moment but you really are. Oh, you'll be sore as hell and you'll have to sleep on your side for a couple of weeks, but you're going to be all right, practically as good as new."

"Max," I said. "Max." I touched his ear, massaged it between my thumb and finger.

Dr. Sanders got to his feet and moved around the table to his medicine cabinet. "I'll give you something for the pain—something to help keep him quiet. You'll give him four of these a day." He was counting out pills, chuting them into the packet, sealing it, labeling it, handing it to me.

"I want Max grounded, absolutely grounded for the next two weeks, And if there is any coughing up of blood, any at all, or if his stool looks bright red or dark in color, you get him over here to Alexandria pronto."

Dr. Sanders held the door and I motioned to Max. Max cried out as he moved, but once underway, he staggered on to the car. At the car I opened the door and Max eyed the seat, looked from it to me—he couldn't climb. I stooped and lifted him, steadied him until he took a leaning stance, his body upright against the back of the seat. He whimpered and rested his cheek on mine. I closed the door carefully and got in the driver's seat and drove at school-zone speed back to Granville.

Being a convalescing patient was not Max's notion of what a dog's life should be. Taking drugs four times a day was not his notion of what a respectable hound would do. The first night he stood before his couch and tried to climb, using first his left leg and then his right. Each time the pain stopped him. He turned to me and waited, accepted my lifting him; I spread my arms wide so that his neck and his back legs took most of the pressure. Once on the couch on his side he lay in place and hardly shifted a muscle throughout the evening. After the eleven o'clock news I gave him his fourth pain pill, and then helped him to his water pan where he drank at most half a dozen laps. From the water pan he went to the back door and waited. I let him out onto the patio. Looking back at me, as if to beg my pardon for what he was about to do—so near the house—he urinated without lifting a leg.

During the night I checked him several times and found him in the position I had helped him to on the couch. He lay on his side, his breathing alternately labored and fast, not quite a breath, not quite a pant. In the morning he went through the same routine, accepting another pill, another trip to the water pan and the patio. I was at school during the day, but Jeanne told me the pattern was much the same at noon. That evening he ate a bite or two of dog food but refused the pill until I buried it in a parcel of the meatloaf Jeanne had baked for our dinner.

After dinner that second day I settled down across from Max who remained in place on his couch. I read a magazine but kept an eye on him, for I had observed that his body movements have become trembly, unsure. Suddenly the trembling grew violent and before I got to him he lunged off the couch, staggering, disoriented, his eyes staring vacantly. As I called Jeanne to come help, he fell into an epileptic seizure. During the three or four minutes the seizure ran its course, I held him, reassuring him as best I could. When he became conscious he began to tremble involuntarily, as if terribly cold. Jeanne brought one of my woolen gardening shirts and I draped it over him and tucked it around him where he lay on his side on the rug. I went to the phone and tried to call Dr. Sanders but got only the answering machine.

Throughout the night I kept a close watch on Max where he slept beneath my gardening shirt, arousing him twice to give him another pain pill. In the morning I began to feel a bit groggy myself, but Max seemed much better. I had gone to the kitchen for a cup of coffee leaving him asleep on the floor, when I heard a leathery shuffling on the kitchen tile and found him headed to his feed bowl.

"Well Max!" I said.

In the bedroom Jeanne heard me and called, "What is it?"

"He's up, he's here at his feed bowl—eating—seems almost ravenous."

Jeanne came to behold him. "Aren't you the one," she cried "Max, you darling."

Max finished his meal with a long drink, and then calmly turned to accept Jeanne's hug. He turned to me and gave me a passing nudge, reconsidered, ran his chin back and forth on my leg, and walked slowly toward the door.

I opened the door and he stepped out onto the patio. When he got to where he had urinated the previous two days he paused, looked back, and then as if saying I can do better, went on, going to the end of the grape arbor before making his toilet.

That morning Jeanne got Dr. Sanders on the phone and described Max's seizure, its duration and his behavior since. Dr. Sanders said such an occurrence was possibly a response to trauma or possibly a side effect of the medication itself, an allergic reaction. He advised to continue the medication but to bring Max to his office at once if he suffered another such attack. He gave Jeanne his home phone number, just in case. "But he's going to be all right," he repeated to Jeanne. "Max is a tough old hound and he's going to be all right."

That day Max stayed on his couch, stayed in place asleep all morning, Jeanne said, and then in the afternoon, made pretty much his usual idiosyncratic moves on the couch, alternating from one end to the other, resting his chin on one arm but never on the other.

Jeanne and I considered that night crucial. We shared with Max a good portion of the warmed over meatloaf in addition to wrapping each pain pill in meatloaf, and the night passed without incident. I slept in my bed that night for the first time since his injury, and when I got up for breakfast Max was already at his feed bowl. After his breakfast Max went out the back door, crossed the patio, and passed the grape arbor, disappearing from sight as he preferred to do to go to his toilet.

I waited a few minutes and whistled once; he promptly returned to take his place for the day, uttering only a slight cry of pain as he climbed onto his couch. Jeanne reported he again slept through the day, and when I came home from school it was evident he was on the mend, that as Dr. Sanders said, he would be all right, barring another epileptic seizure, which did not occur.

Warning Signs

The sedative pills Dr. Sanders had counted out lasted Max two weeks and one day. I'm sure they contributed substantially to his accepting his being grounded as a necessary evil, one to be tolerated with as much grace as possible. During that interval, to the best of my knowledge, he had only two meetings with Wolfgang, both at their trysting spot, both with Max on leash. The meetings lasted at most five or ten minutes—while I was talking to the Zimmers, explaining that Max was indisposed and under the care of Dr. Sanders. I did not mention the cause of his illness and I'm not sure how much information about his injury and its perpetrator Max communicated to Wolfgang.

That Max gave considerable thought to Wolfgang during this period of separation, I'm reasonably sure. During the tenth day of his enforced idleness, when I came from school, I discovered my note-taking clipboard had disappeared from its customary resting place on the corner of the coffee table. I saw it lying face down under Max's couch, but I gave it no thought, assuming that it had got knocked off the overloaded coffee table and had somehow been pushed to it present location, possibly when Jeanne was vacuuming the rug.

I picked up the clipboard with its attached yellow legal pad, straightened the slightly wrinkled first page of the pad, and placed the clipboard back on the coffee table. When I discovered the clipboard in the same spot beneath Max's couch the following day I again picked it up, and this time I riffled through the wrinkled outer pages—straightening them really—only to discover the following half page in a script that seemed modeled on Jeanne's handwriting:

Toward The Education Of Wolfgang Zimmer

1. How many animals can *live* on the head of a pin?
2. Is Horace Greeley's counsel "Go west, young dog, go west," still sound?
3. Since most of us want to move up in the world, what direction should we take?
4. What do you want to be when you aren't what you are?

P.S. Wolfgang, since you need answer *only three* of these questions to achieve fundamental literacy in this funky world, which *one* will you omit?

My first thought was that Jeanne had been jotting notes while playing make-believe with Max—some game she might have devised to occupy his fanciful mind while his body was grounded. My second thought was *not so fast,* this recuperation has some days to run.

Glancing to see that Max was asleep—as he appeared to be—I replaced the clipboard on the coffee table and went about my mundane business of grading thirty-two blue books, the result of an hour examination I had given in American literature.

But you can bet I kept an eye on the clipboard with its yellow legal pad. And the next day, the instant I entered the room, I saw the clipboard. Somehow it had, once again, managed to fall from the coffee table and get pushed beneath Max's couch. I couldn't get to it unobserved that evening but I did the second, while Max was in the kitchen eating his evening meal. I listened for the jingle of his name tag and license against his feed bowl, then I flipped through the yellow sheets.

Sure enough, there was a new set of jottings in a hand that matched the first:

Notions To Ponder on a Squirrel Hunt

1. If you must strike while the iron is hot, what kind of clock are you?
2. What do you see beyond the horizon?
3. Will peace endure?
4. Why war?
5. What is time?
6. What time is it when it is time to?

Slowly I reread the questions to make sure I had read them correctly. Then I became aware that the jingle of metal on bowl had stopped. I barely got the clipboard and its yellow legal pad back *under the couch* before Max entered the room.

That night Jeanne went to bed at her usual ten o'clock, and I lingered till 3 a.m. to finish grading my American literature papers and to keep an eye on Max. He was well along in his recovery except for the inevitable gasp of pain in getting on or off his couch. When I finally went to bed Jeanne heard me and stirred in her sleep. Thinking this was my chance, I whispered: "Could I ask you a question: have you been writing those strange questions on the yellow legal pad attached to the clipboard?"

"Max," Jeanne murmured, "please. You've done nothing but talk questions. . .questions. . .ques—"

She was not awake, and I sensed it would be a mean thing to arouse her with a question about questions. Besides, I decided I could confront her with the legal pad itself in the morning. Pulling the alarm on our bedside clock I crawled into bed.

Sometime between three and 7:30 a.m. I thought I heard Jeanne get out of bed and enter the living room. I thought I heard her talking to Max and I could have sworn I heard her reading off the following:

Toward the Education of a Middle-aged Marine

1. Are you you or are you your brother?
2. Who is *your* father?
3. Will the sun shine ever?
4. What is love?
5. When will *it* rain? reign? rein?
6. Why man?
7. Why, man?

P.S. Speak to Wolfgang of the power of the comma, the latent perfection in the question mark.

P.P.S. It is possible, not easy but possible, to grow older *and* wiser.

The alarm zinged its cheery call. Still in my pajamas I went to the clipboard where it lay beneath Max's couch. With it in hand I entered the kitchen.

"Hon," I said, "did you write these questions on my legal pad?" I was riffling through the yellow pad as Jeanne replied:

"Didn't you ask me that silly question last night, and didn't you preface it with a sillier one: could I ask you a question? And didn't you wake me from a sound sleep to ask me that?"

"I just—" I stared in disbelief at the legal pad in my hand. It was blank. Again I riffled through the pages. Every page was blank. I tried it page by page, working through to the cardboard backing. Nothing. I unfastened the legal pad from the clipboard and carefully examined the gummed edge—ah, the pad separated into two parts, as it would do if someone had removed pages completely and in the process had broken the gum seal that held the pages together.

Jeanne was saying: "If there was something written on that legal pad, it's still there. Don't stand there like a ninny staring at two sections of a legal pad as if you've just lost your last friend. PB, wake up."

"I just don't know what to think," I said. "I"d have sworn—well, never mind."

Jeanne went to the bedroom. She returned and handed me my robe. "You'd better eat and get underway." Her voice softened: "I'll take care of Max."

Hearing his name, Max got off the couch. I heard him utter his little cry of pain, and then I heard his leathery footpads striking the kitchen floor tile. In peripheral vision I watched him carefully. He cast a side-long glance at me, giving special heed to the legal pad and clipboard I held in my hand.

I turned to him but he looked away, pretended to become very interested in his feed bowl.

"Yes. You do that—you take care of Max," I said to Jeanne.

That ended—should have ended—Max's recuperative writing, but when living with Max I have learned to expect an extra, in writing it would be an extra chapter. I read it that evening when I came home from school and found the clipboard and legal pad lying *under the couch.* I saw it there the instant I entered the living room and I could plainly see something written on the legal pad's uncurled first page. Although Max responded to my greeting with a "hmmn" and Jeanne said "hi," I could sense they were waiting like two chipmunks poised on high legs.

"Well," I said, sitting down on the couch and reaching for the clipboard, "I see our seancing friend has penned a little message."

Max and Jeanne showed amazement. Max twisted his head, Jeanne said, "Really."

I straightened the curled yellow sheet and read: "This is the other side."

Intrigued and not wishing to appear as clumsy and

dense as some men might in such a situation, I calmly but quickly turned the yellow sheet over and straightened it. There I read: "This is the other side."

This time there was no doubt about the authorship, for beneath each sign there was a paw print. I glanced from one smiling face to the other.

"You two hounds, you two subtle, loving hounds!"

Danger

Because Max was grounded and I knew where he had been night and day for two weeks I was not at all prepared for the telephone call I received that Saturday afternoon. The caller was Dr. Wesley Carouthers, who had taught at Denison for thirteen years. A widely published psychologist of Skinnerian bent, and a descendant of the Cadwalladers of Alabama and the Lees of Virginia, Dr. Carouthers tempered scientific knowledge with southern charm. Here is our conversation:

Dr. Carouthers: I don't like to have to bother you about this, Paul, but I have to report that your dog attacked me.

PB: My dog attacked you? Max attacked you?

Dr. Carouthers: Your big German shepherd. About nine or nine thirty this morning when I was jogging past your house he sprang out from under a yew bush. I tried to fend him off but he was mad as hell, growling, slobbering, gnashing. Using my old Georgia Tech broken field running tactics I dodged his first tackle and took off up the road but he overtook me from behind. Tore the ass out of my running suit, and took a sizeable—

PB: Wesley, Wesley, Max is not a big German shepherd. He is half shepherd but he looks more like a hound, sort of black and tan.

Dr. Carouthers: Then who owns the big German shepherd? He was lying concealed under the yew bush just beyond your mail box and he sure as hell seemed to be waiting on me. He let six or eight students go right by, and then when he saw me coming he leaped out—like he was a damned griffin flying out to take part in some mythological war. He sure sank his fangs in my ham, tore the ass right out of my running suit, like I said.

PB: My god Wesley, I'm sorry to hear this. Have you seen a doctor, did you require stitches?

Dr. Carouthers: I've seen Doc Summers. He's stitched my backside together with his baseball stitches but says I've got to locate the dog. On account of the possibility of rabies, all that crap. You don't know who owns a German shepherd that looks like a German shepherd, only larger? I have to take the damned rabies treatment if I don't find the dog.

PB: I'm not at all sure—

Dr. Carouthers: This is not the first time I've been bit. Once when I was in the military one of the damned guard dogs took a dislike to me for reasons I never did understand. He took a hold of my right knee like he meant to tear my leg off. I've still got scars to show for that encounter. You don't know anybody there on Burg Street that owns a German shepherd?

PB: Well, our neighbors, the Zimmers, own a German shepherd. But he's the world's last dog to be vicious, I mean really bite someone. The poor bastard's been neutered and he's given to whimpering and crying—sort of a Faulknerian Benjy looking for Caddy, you know. He wouldn't even attack a baby. He might attack another dog but not a person, not a—"

Dr. Carouthers: Not a psychologist you were about to say? I don't think the dog that nipped my ass would know a psychologist from a T-bone steak. What's that family's name again?

PB: Zimmer. Their dog's Wolfgang, but names can be damned misleading, as you know.

Dr. Carouthers: You don't have to teach English or psychology to know that. Well, I'm right sorry I bothered you, Paul. I'll give this Zimmer family a call about this just in case it was their dog that nailed me. I'd know him in a minute, not that I'd want to get close enough to identify him.

PB: I'm just—almost—sure it couldn't be Wolfgang.

Dr. Carouthers: I'll check it out. And again, I'm danged sorry I called to bother you about it.

PB: Wesley, before you hang up—What branch of the military were you in. It wasn't the Marines by any chance?

Dr. Carouthers: How the hell did you guess? I've never made it top secret but I've never spread it around either. To tell the truth I was once a hard-ass sergeant at Camp Le Jeune, one of those who marched his platoon straight up the halls of Montezuma—all that. When I got out and read a little psychology and got into grad school I shoved all that stuff where it belongs.

PB: But I'll bet you've still got the Marine—well, the scent.

Dr. Carouthers: Paul, you're into something—would you care to tell me what?

PB: Wesley, if I told you—if I so much as hinted at it—you'd have me over there in your department doing pigeon tricks.

Dr. Carouthers: You damned English teachers—always hinting and then asking who's pointing? Paul, I'm sorry as hell I troubled you—almost accused you—that tone. You understand?

PB: Of course. Wesley I'm sorrier than I can say that you got bit. Take care now and I'll see you around.

Dr. Carouthers: Righto. Hey Paul, what's your dog's name again?

PB: Max.

Dr. Carouthers: Tell Max I wasn't really accusing him. I just didn't know.

PB: He'll understand. He'll be damned sorry—I mean *damned sorry*—that you got bit. Take care, Wesley.

Dr. Carouthers: You too, Paul.

An Ordeal

It was another Saturday in May, and Jeanne and Max and I traveled by station wagon south on Interstate 77. We were headed to Marietta, almost one hundred miles south-southeast of Granville, not because it was Jeanne's hometown, as it was, but because it had once been the garden spot of Ohio. And even after being taken over and jam-packed with chemical plants during and following World War II, it was, we knew, still a good source of garden plants.

Our immediate mission was to buy a few hundred sizeable tomato plants, as many as the station wagon would hold, to replace the twelve hundred plants we had raised from seed and nourished with tender loving care from February 1 to Thursday of the week just past. On Thursday—white Thursday—we had lost in the field our entire crop of sturdy plants. Most already bore one cluster of yellow flowers, some a cluster of green fruit and a second cluster of blossoms, but by a quirk of the weather the entire crop had been frozen solid, turned to nauseous green jelly, in a late May frost.

I was thinking when the world turns sour it rots, and

when it rots it takes on that noxious odor gardeners associate with decay in the cabbage family: broccoli, Brussels sprouts, cauliflower, kale, kohlrabi, rape, rutabaga, turnips—the whole *Brassica* clan.

"It would be funny—bizarre funny—if it weren't so sad," Jeanne remarked.

"The tomatoes," I said. "Ah, easy come, easy go, eh, Max? After all. the three of us spent only a couple hundred hours planting the seed, transplanting, hardening off, setting them out, tying them to the stakes, not to mention working the ground, pounding the stakes. The farmer's lot is like the fisherman's luck—"

"Which is?"

"A wet ass and a hungry gut."

"Round one for visceral Irish wit," Jeanne said dryly. "But is it wit at all?"

"Your saying that restores my faith in Father," I said. "Strange how I think of him at such times. He used that description of fisherman's luck as an example of wit marred by vulgarity. But I sort of liked it—for a time like this."

There was a slight stir in the back seat and Max groaned.

"Max agrees with your father," Jeanne said. "And you know darned well I was *not* talking about tomatoes. The Zimmers feel they just have to do something with dear old Wolfgang."

"They just have to keep him close—tie him up till the quarantine is over. Where is he now?"

"He's tied in their garage, has been since the attack."

"Not tied with a chain? He snaps chains like rubber

bands. I hope they know better than that.

"He's tied in their garage with the nylon webbing Buddy got when he bought all that surplus Army gear." Jeanne touched the seat belt looped across her breast.

"Seat-belt strong?" I asked.

"Seat-belt strong," Jeanne added: "They don't even allow him off his nylon tether to go to the toilet. He has to go right there in the garage. Poor dear."

I glanced at Jeanne and saw tears in her eyes.

"Hon," I said, "you've heard something more?"

"Ruby said they are considering taking him to a vet, having him put to sleep."

"Kill him—they wouldn't do that!"

"They feel they have to. Now that he's actually attacked someone, done physical damage."

Neither Jeanne nor I spoke for some time. On the back seat Max got to his feet, giving a little cry of pain as he did so. I waited for a second cry that would indicate he had resettled himself. It didn't come.

"Is *he* all right?" I asked.

Jeanne turned and looked. "He's just standing up. He's all right."

"Sit down, Max," I said. "Sit down." I waited and then repeated the command. There came a slight yipe, and Jeanne said, "He's lying down again." She felt in her purse for her handkerchief.

The only sound in the car was the hum of the motor, the whirr of tires on concrete, the sound of occasional gusts of wind—the sky was overcast, it was more March than late May. Finally I said:

"If it had to happen, it's good it was Wesley Carouthers and not some jerk who'd get a lawyer and sue the Zimmers blind."

"Rob them blind is the cliche," Jeanne said.

"Do you suppose Max really played a part in it?" I asked.

"That's what I meant by *bizarre funny,*" Jeanne said. "But then I say to myself, be realistic, how could he?"

"You know Max." I paused. "He and Wolfgang are thick as—is it thiev—?" I stopped as Jeanne punched me. But she was almost smiling, and I'd trade a worked up cliche for a smile from Jeanne any day.

I said: "At least you and I know Max is capable of it. He not only understands English, he intuits what's not been said."

"I'd believe it if Max himself did something untoward."

"You mean bite somebody?"

"He'd never do that. I mean something out of character. I'm not sure what it might be, but I'd know it if it happened."

"Womanly intuition?" I said. "You'll tell me when."

Jeanne was silent, then she turned to Max. "I'd know," she said. "Right, Max?"

"We'd probably all know," I said. "And don't you be getting any ideas, Max. You hear me?"

"He just rolled an eye toward you," Jeanne reported. A moment later she said: "You want to know what I really think—"

"I tried to ask you about three o'clock a.m. a week or ten days ago. I got a gentle rebuff."

Jeanne smiled and went on: "I think what happened—what that Randy Neighbor character did to Max and what Wolfgang did to Wesley Carouthers—proves violence operates on a very fixed law."

"You sound like a physicist. You really think that?"

"Why else would such gentle, kind-hearted people as the Zimmers be considering putting dear old Wolfgang to sleep? Violence breeds violence whether done by persons, animals, nations—in any name whatsoever."

"I hadn't thought of it that way."

"Do think of it that way."

We were turning off the Interstate at Exit 1 to enter downtown Marietta.

We drove a few blocks west on Greene Street which parallels the Ohio River. Our destination was the lunch room of the Lafayette Motor Inn, a remodeled hotel built on the point of land where the Muskingum River joins the Ohio. A bronze plaque in the parking lot informed us this was the spot where the French General Lafayette, of Revolutionary War fame, had disembarked from a riverboat during his last visit to the United States in 1825.

We set Max free on the riverbank. He walked gingerly, left his mark, and returned to the car. I locked the door behind him. Jeanne and I entered the Lafayette's "Gun Room," a name we found revolutionary for a dining hall, where we enjoyed a delicious, leisurely lunch, topped off with oxheart cherry sundaes.

After lunch I stopped off in the Men's Room and Jeanne went directly to the car. When I emerged from the Men's Room Jeanne was re-entering the lobby. Her face told me she had news, impossible news.

"Prepare yourself," she exclaimed, "prepare yourself for something beyond belief." She motioned toward the parking lot. "Something that will shake you, hurt you."

"Maxie—has something happened to him?" I was all but running, struggling into my jacket, fumbling for my car keys.

Then I stood at the window above Max. He was curled into a ball on his plaid blanket. I pecked on the window; he barely raised an eyebrow, opened one eye.

I turned to Jeanne. "You mean he's sleeping in a ball, no longer sleeping on his side? That's a damned good sign. Boy, you had me scared!" I got my key into the lock but found the door unlocked, she *had been* to the car.

She said: "He's acting."

"So what?" I said. "He's acting—I'm acting, you're acting. We're all acting—eating, sleeping, breathing. I thought you had discovered something—"

I moved around the car. Jeanne leaned across and unlocked my door. I opened it and stood staring at what Jeanne had discovered: the seat belt was cut straight across as if by a razor. It was cut not once but twice. As I stared, unbelieving, Jeanne held out her seat belt, it was cut in a similar straight line but cut only once.

"What the—?" I began. "Was it vandals—was the car unlocked when you got to it?"

"The car was locked. It was not vandals," Jeanne nodded toward the back seat.

"Did you see it?"

"Of course not. But you ask him."

"Maxie," I said, "did you cut these seat belts?"

Without moving his head in the least Max opened both eyes, rolled them until the whites showed, a gesture he used often to show empty pockets: "What did you say? Were you by any chance talking to me?"

I turned to Jeanne. "He couldn't do it. He *could not* do it. Thcsc belts have been cut with a razor, or a sharp knife. I'll bet someone—"

Jeanne held up her severed belt and said, "At least you concede they are cut. They were not cut when we unsnapped them, when we left the car and locked it."

I was fingering the new edge of black nylon. Did I feel a bit of moisture or was it my imagination? "Well," I said, "there's one way we might find out." I opened the door and crouched above Max. I lifted his head and said, "You open your mouth, Mister."

He struggled, twisting his head aside, but I jammed my fingers into his mouth and felt along his gums on the left side, lower and upper, thinking as I did so, "Max, forgive me, forgive me."

Nothing! For an instant my finger probed the cutting edges of his upper back teeth—razor sharp—then he jerked his head free, opening his mouth to dislodge my finger without crushing it. As he did so I saw it, a black thread wedged into the shining white ridge of teeth on the right side of his mouth. I grabbed his head, pinned it to the seat, pushed the lip back and yanked out the inch-long black thread. I held it up for Jeanne to see.

"Well," she said, "that's one mystery solved."

"Max, I should give you a belting! I mean a lamming! I mean a real thumping!" Seizing his neck ruff I yanked him toward me. My right hand had automatically shaped itself into a fist. Max cowered, his body began to tremble and he strove to get to his feet but I held him in place.

"PB," Jeanne cried, "are you Randy Neighbor?"

Her words got to me. Slowly I released my grip, unclenched my fist. Max glanced to my face, then eyed the wall of his seat as if debating whether he might risk scrambling for the back end of the station wagon, anything to escape his mad attacker.

Jeanne said: "You and I brought this on ourselves. We told him about Wolfgang. You yourself asked if the nylon that holds him was—how did you put it—seat-belt strong?"

I said: "This is beyond—beyond—"

Jeanne said: "Just leave it there. That's where it belongs."

I felt sick to my stomach. Slowly I reached out to Max. He trembled but accepted my hand. I moved my hand from his head to his ear, to his cheek. He hesitated, then raised his nose to my hand, tentatively touched it with his tongue. I got out, closed his door, and edged behind the wheel.

"Thanks," I said to Jeanne. I started the motor, thinking it felt strange not to be hooking up a seat belt.

We left the lot and drove up Front Street to the Muskingum River bridge. We crossed the bridge and drove north alongside the Muskingum to the Littlefield Garden Center, which happened to lie directly across the river from the house where Jeanne had grown up. This garden spot held a special place in her heart. During all her growing years it had been her view, her route to the horizon and whatever the future held. In every season, in all weathers, she had pondered these fields, these trees, this expanse of sky from her own flower garden, or at a higher angle, from her own bedroom.

She and I stood for a moment looking across to the

backyard where I had first encountered her in Marietta. We had met at Ohio University in Athens, Ohio, the spring of 1939, and that August I borrowed my brother's pickup truck and drove to Marietta. When I rang at the front door of her house, her mother answered the door. I introduced myself and she said: "Jeanne's out back working with her flowers." She motioned. I went down the walk, around the house, across the yard and came upon a tall beautiful flower among many. A flower who through the years has found more ways of saying yes that the sun itself.

I wanted to say something of what I felt to Jeanne, but I was too close to my recent behavior to speak. She understood—as she always does—for she smiled and said softly: "This is the other side."

I touched her hand. "Let's go see what Littlefield has in tomatoes."

They had exactly the varieties we had hoped for: Early Girl, Moreton Hybrid, Big Boy, Jubilee. Early, midseason, and late reds, a fine variety of yellow. The plants weren't as far advanced as those we had raised from seed, but they were thrifty, well-rooted plants, and they could be had at a reasonable price. We put down Max's seat and loaded the entire bed of the station wagon with flat after flat, placing the last two flats in the front, one to rest on the seat between Jeanne and me, the other under her feet.

I didn't want to take the last two flats but Jeanne insisted, knowing we had at best only half the usual crop in prospect with all the plants we could haul. I didn't want Jeanne to sit straddling that flat for a hundred mile drive but as Jeanne often says, she's a tough old bird equal to almost anything life can toss at her. She insisted we take the last two flats, and we did.

In loading the back of the wagon we had left Max only a one-flat niche of space on the floor next to the many plants. His slightest shift of position would have crushed countless tender green stems, but he too understood our need and held himself like a statue during the hundred mile drive back to Granville. *When you get right down to it*—to use a phrase my father often used when he wanted to assert a truth—Max and Jeanne had much in common in addition to having to put up with me. Their's was a rare kind of toughness.

Labors of Love

Jeanne and Max and I labored steadily and happily much of Sunday afternoon and Monday after school to set out our 624 new tomato plants, to transfer them from their thirteen plastic flats to their permanent garden home. Such a task required of the three of us much of what in gardening is called "stoop labor," a term some non-gardeners think refers to the mentality of those who work the earth. We dug holes and we filled those holes with water; we wet down the plants in their flats and then lifted out each plant with infinite care; we placed each plant in its water-feathered home, firming down the finest soil around its hair roots; we then again blessed each plant with holy water, and we prayed throughout.

Those movements of ritual we carried out with quiet joy: to let each plant know we cared, and caring we wanted it to thrive, to take on its distinctive shape, to become one with earth and sky and sun. In such major undertakings one's back does learn to bend, and sometimes takes on a bent, not of subservience but of life's give-and-take; one's hands wax large and harden and callous, the better to handle and hold fast the flame latent in the earth.

As Jeanne and I did our thing, Max did his. Most of Sunday afternoon he gardened with his usual gusto, except he made no spectacular runs. He did his usual conscientious row work, inspecting each and every growing row, walking rather than loping as had been his custom. He deigned to "mouth" and drag a few tomato stakes wherever they had to be reset. He did his share of digging, stiff-legged but earth moving, most of it beneath the pile of unused tomato stakes where his mobile black rubber nose, pushed to the stakes, told him there was a toad, a field mouse, or a garden snake, or possibly all three.

Several times during Sunday afternoon I noticed Max left the work at hand and went to his and Wolfgang's trysting spot. There he stood, looking off toward the Zimmer house, the Zimmer garage. His head on point, looking and listening, he waited several minutes each time and then came back to Jeanne or to me to ask if we knew why Wolfgang wasn't out and about. Late in the afternoon he ventured into Wolfgang's territory, went so far as the Zimmer grape arbor, and paused there, whimpering, questioning.

This time I called him sharply and he returned promptly, but faced away when he got to my side, looking off toward what I knew to be Wolfgang's prison.

Night was coming on, and Jeanne and I began gathering up the empty flats, the tools, the water buckets—all the paraphernalia of our labors. Max sensed we were going in and he dashed back to the trysting spot and then returned to us, possibly trying to suggest that we go home that way around. Jeanne and I moved on. Max hung back and I had to speak to him, tell him to come along now.

I went so far as to say what I didn't think but had to say: "Wolfgang's going to be all right. Don't you worry, things always work out. He's going to be all right."

And Max knew what I uttered was hogwash. He stopped, settled on his haunches, reared his head straight back, pointed his nose to the shadowing sky and gave forth a series of long-draw-out piercing wails. The sound ranged to the hills, echoed there, mounted to the sky. It sent eerie shivers up and down my spine. Jeanne stopped as if stricken.

The echo of Max's keening wail had barely died when we heard an answering set of wails from what had to be the Zimmer' garage. Those wails sounded every bit as keen but a trifle less plaintive. Perhaps they were tempered by the distance, perhaps their owner was more reconciled to what he faced.

That exchange, of a kind beyond human understanding, was to be the last Wolfgang and Max would make to each other on this earth.

On Monday evening when we went to finish planting the remainder of the tomato plants, Max moved directly to the trysting spot and stood there looking off to the Zimmer garage. He stood a long time with his umbrella ears raised. I watched him closely, thinking from his posture he was ready to dash off in that direction. He seemed puzzled by what his ears told him. Several times he shifted his head and sniffed the air, testing the slight breeze coming from the east. Finally he turned and stood looking off toward the walnut woods, staring into its shadows where he and Wolfgang had often run neck against neck in a rousing race to surprise and drive into the trees the foxes and grays. Finally he turned and came back to me, stood before me.

I spoke to him and he seemed pleased I had done so. He

moved close enough that his shoulder brushed my knee. When I moved down the tomato row he stayed closed beside me.

In the dusk, when we were putting our gardening tools away in the garage, Ruby and Rudolph Zimmer passed the end of our driveway on one of their many evening strolls. They paused to speak to us, and Max waltzed out to greet them. Perhaps he posed an unspoken question, for Ruby Zimmer turned and walked up the drive to us. Her voice was happy-sad.

"We've taken Wolfgang away. We found a farm family that wants him. They have a twelve year old son—"

"Thank God," Jeanne murmured. "Thank God."

"Their son wants, needs, a dog. They live on a dairy farm out west of Alexandria; we took him over last night."

"I though he might be gone," I said. "Max seemed to feel it."

"We're so happy," Ruby Zimmer said. "Wolfgang is safe."

Jeanne spoke to Ruby to comfort her—and to be comforted.

"Hear that," I said to Max. "Wolfgang's gone to a farm out west of Alexandria. He'll have a boy to play with. He'll have his own barnyard to play in, farm fields to roam over."

My words rolled on but they were wasted on Max. He looked up at me in sorrow and I could read his eyes: Wolfgang is gone from me forever, and to be gone forever—what is death?

Changes

Now came a moonlit October evening in another year. Classes were well begun at Denison, and Jeanne and I had settled into a routine that kept Max close to home throughout the day but allowed him to make runs at night, runs that often necessitated my driving his bus to campus about midnight. Usually I would find him on the quad between the Union and Fellows Hall, or in inclement weather, in the Union lobby.

Jeanne and I often spoke of the changes a couple years had made: the gains, the losses, the holding of one's own against time's larceny. For Max the changes were mostly gains; his wounded chest had completely healed, he ran and pranced and played with abandon. In doing so his every action set man and animals at ease: "I've seldom met a worser hound than I; join me in my Maxish way."

Some of his losses could be read as gains. Within weeks of Wolfgang's disappearance Max's muzzle had turned gray, leaving him even more distinguished. Exactly when his black nose got dipped in white, neither Jeanne nor I could say. He was lying on his couch attending to our conversation one evening when Jeanne said: "Look at his muzzle." I did. It was gray. "When did that happen?" Jeanne asked. I couldn't tell her. I could and did wonder at what price each of those gray hairs was bought.

There was another loss, a real loss, yet it too recorded as a non-event. Max no longer walnuted. Not once since the morning Randy Neighbor drove his knee into his chest had Max lain out on his back saying to the world: Here I am, I am the open one, look at me, look at me! I took that loss of trust as the judgment it was.

We had credited Max with teaching Wolfgang to walnut, and Jeanne missed the Wolfgang walnut as much as I missed those of Max. One early morning while weighing zucchini for market in the hanging scale in the garage she stumbled and set the scale swaying, the zucchini tumbling, as if for the instant her vision had blurred. I caught her, steadied her, and helped her collect the fallen vegetables. She said, "It's nothing," but I saw it was something hurtful.

A week or so later as we were settling into bed she remarked: "That morning at the scale—"

"Yes."

"It just suddenly hit me. There would never again be one of those mornings when Max and I would step into the garage to start our walk and find Wolfgang walnuting under the scale, his great body laid out, his yellow legs in stiff-arm, stretched high against the wall. He'd have been there since shortly after dawn waiting to be discovered and exclaimed over. Often I'd hear him arrive at dawn, announce himself at our window here, whimper softly, and go shuffling off to settle down in the garage. Sometimes I'd hear his legs as he swung them aloft and let them thud against the wall to begin his waiting, his walnuting."

There were other changes, too. The Neighbors, Henrietta and Henry and Max's friend Betsy, had moved to Alaska. "The neighborly Neighbors are shipping out of your neighborhood," Henry is said to have announced. When Jeanne told me that news I put in Max's two cents' worth: "For the sake of all malamutes and friendly wolves I hope the forty-ninth state is off limits for Henry's younger brother."

"You know of course that the Neighbors' house has finally sold?" Jeanne was saying. She had lingered past her usual bedtime to watch the rerun of a Lincoln Center performance on TV, and I had just entered the living room from the kitchen where I'd been reading and marking a set of Advanced Composition papers.

"It's been bought by a family from South Carolina, a family named Colburn, Elaine and Alexander Colburn. He's a physicist out at Owens-Corning Tech Center."

"Where do you get all this information?" I asked. "You spend every free minute walking Max, but you have a pipeline to the world that Ben Bradlee of *The Washington Post* would envy."

Jeanne smiled. "I listen to little Renee Corbett. When she joins Max and me on our walks. Or if she misses us on the walks, when we come by where she's waiting on her school bus. She reports the news as it should be reported: 'Mrs. B., do you know—Mrs. B., have you heard—' and there it is: factual, clear, delightful."

"She could report a great story on me," I said.

"On the Colburns she says, 'The have a Great Dame

dog—just in case you see *her* running with Max. She's black like Max, and nice, but she's much bigger. She's registered. Her name is Carolina Belle, but she comes if you call her Carrie or if you call her Belle.'"

"A Great Dame—a registered Great Dame—deserves two names," I said.

"What story would Renee have to tell on you?" Jeanne asked.

"I couldn't do it justice," I said. "Only Max or Renee could do that. When next you see Renee ask about the time she babysat with Max and me while I redid the mailbox. She'll remember, I'm sure"

"You won't tell?" Jeanne said.

"You ask Renee."

"Well I'm off to bed without my bedtime story," Jeanne said. "If Max were here, I'd lodge a complaint." Without regret she moved to the stairs.

I sat remembering. It was in July that our mailbox had been destroyed for the third time in three years, and this time the vandals didn't merely wham the box from a car, they stopped and took the mailbox with them. Left with only a post, and it splintered and shaky on its moorings, I talked the situation over with Max and we decided to get a new box *and* a new post.

We did. Max went with me on our rounds. We went to the Granville Hardware for a new box and we stopped at the Granville Milling and bought an eight inch locust post, a well-seasoned locust post. Max and I did our measuring and sawing and prepping, and after a couple hours work we had the mailbox firmly affixed to the locust post, the whole unit ready to slip into the ground.

I had removed the old splintered post and was busy with the post-hole digger, enlarging and deepening the hole, when a bicycle came speeding down the road being ridden by a tiny mite whose cheery "Hello Mr. B." identified Renee Corbett.

"Hi Renee."

The rider nimbly stepped off the bicycle letting it fall into the gravel of the drive.

"What are you doing, Mr. B.?"

"I'm trying to set in this new mailbox."

"Would you want me to babysit with Max? While you work?"

"That would be nice. He would like that."

Renee danced over and sat down next to Max, who lay in the shade of the apple tree, supervising my every move. She settled close to Max and straightened out her print dress. "I'm your baby sitter," she announced. Max turned to mouth her hand. Renee got up and said: "I think I'll babysit from the other side."

She moved to the opposite side of Max, took the same position, and carefully straightened out her dress. She spoke to Max and moved a trifle closer to him. They began a game. She held out a fallen apple twig and he reached for it. She snatched it away, and then held it out again, and he reached for it.

I worked away with the digger. In short order I had the hole deep enough—I measured it twice—and measured the post. All was just right.

Lifting the post with mailbox affixed I slid it into the hole, straightened it there, and steadied it with one hand while I pushed enough dirt into the hole to support the post upright. Once the post was steady in place I let go of it and took up my shovel to fill the hole. I had thrown in three or four shovelfuls of dirt and begun to tamp it in place when Renee spoke:

"Mr. B.?"

"Yes."

"Mr. B., I don't know if I should tell you this, but you've got the mailbox backward."

I looked. She was right. I fully expected Max to give forth a groan but he merely took his chance to steal the twig from *our* babysitter.

Those are the facts. Renee will tell them better, I'm sure, and Jeanne is entitled to the better version. Thinking it was about time to go for Max, I stepped into the kitchen to get a drink and to check out the clock. I was in the kitchen when the phone rang.

Enroute to the phone I whimsically wondered if I might begin: "Max's bus—Driver speaking," but decided against it.

"Hello,"I said.

"Is this Paul?" began a voice I knew to be that of Mrs. Robinson, who with her husband Victor owned the white pine woods and black angus cattle farm that adjoined our property to the west.

"Yes."

"Well I thought I ought to tell you, Max is down here at our place."

"I thought he'd gone up to the college. He usually does this time of night. I'll drive right down to get him."

"Yes—well." Mrs. Robinson sounded tentative.

"He hasn't done any damage?" I said.

"Oh no. But I'm not sure you should drive—he might damage your car."

"Yes?"

"He's been out in the barnyard mucking around. He's rolled in the fresh cow manure—is really a sight, drippy, smelly."

I sang: "Oh Mrs. Robinson." She laughed and I laughed. Then I said: "Thanks very much for warning me. I'll *walk* right down and get him."

New Adventures

Had the first night of Max's going for a roll in cow manure been his last, I would have thought little of it. As it worked out, I will never forget it. During my Randy Neighbor act in Marietta I had vowed *that* would be the first and last time I would raise a fist against Max, and I meant to keep that vow. Thus there was something almost purgatorial and therapeutic for him and for me in the bath I gave him, as if our spirits were harmonized by the soft October night, the warm southwest breeze. It was a night for the wee folk of Irish myth—we sensed it in our blood. (Was Max's father really an Irish setter?)

After gathering a bar of deodorant soap and three worn but freshly laundered bath towels I drew a tub of lukewarm water for the bath and two buckets of slightly cooler rinse water. Then I stripped down to my shorts, and we bathed on the patio in the moonlight, the time being about 1 a.m.

Max took the bath in the spirit it was offered. He seemed delighted with his having achieved a barnyard fragrance that merited such attention. His gaiety became a rowdiness when he was well lathered, the rowdiness led to a sashaying run around the picnic table, over the retaining wall of the patio, back around the patio and the fireplace, all the while barking at full voice.

When Jeanne called out "What's going on out there?" I thought she referred to our hullabaloo.

"He's the loud one," I responded. "We're bathing by moonlight. You go back to sleep."

"That peculiar odor, that stench I smelled?" Jeanne called.

"Max rolled in manure down at the Robinson barn."

I had recaptured Max and was dumping the first bucket of rinse water over him. Possibly the water was cooler than I thought. Max exploded into a dervish head-to-tail shaking that treated me to a shower of sudsy something that in polite language could be called bovine beer. I stilled the dervish and dumped the second bucket of rinse water, slapping my hands and inviting him to shake and run it off while I repaired to the kitchen for a refill on bath and rinse water. It would take a least two baths to dent that fragrance.

Jeanne, clad in her green velvet housecoat, entered the kitchen bearing two half-gallons of tomato juice, one mason jar under each arm.

"Use these just before the final rinse. Work them well into the fur. Tomato juice will negate the worst of it."

"I used deodorant soap, I was considering using your shampoo. He smells rarer than Wolfgang used to smell at his worst. The deodorant soap didn't touch him."

Jeanne, whose sensitivity to smells rivals Max's, wrinkled her nose as I passed her. "You'll be lucky if deodorant soap will touch *you*."

She held the door for me to carry out the tub. Max, gleaming wet and shiny as a black seal, attempted to wedge his way in through the door.

"Oh no you don't." Jeanne caught him and pushed him back, closed the screen door against him. "You stay outside, you still smell like a barnyard on legs." She raised her hands to her nose and turned to wash them.

"Such talk will encourage him," I said. "He'll be down at the Robinson barn tomorrow night—or sooner." I set the tub down and returned to get the two buckets of rinse water. Are you sure you want me to use the tomato juice?"

"It's the only thing to use, trust your woman," Jeanne said.

"But you slaved over it, worked so hard to can it."

"We've got plenty," she said. "More than you and I will drink. And he earned his share."

Max, now fully into the bathing game, liked the tone of Jeanne's voice, and barked out an order for *his* tomato juice—"two jars full, please!"

"You're determined to encourage him," I said. I grabbed Max and got him to step into the tub, and again lathered him with deodorant soap. The bar was now so haircovered it felt wrapped in straw. "If you do encourage him," I said over my shoulder, "you know who gives the next bath."

The moonlight silvered by Jeanne's laughter, as if I had just delivered one of the world's best jokes. And before I could say "hey" she had stepped out of her green housecoat and was upon Max and me, embracing us both, splashing and laughing.

"Seeing him and you I can't pass up helping on this one."

Then the three of us were splashing and lathering, lathering and laughing, and it was elfin season, In elfin season what sights you scc, what sounds you hear:

> Rubba dub dub, three men in a tub. And one of them isn't a man! One weighs in at seventy-five, one weighs in at one seventy-five, and one weighs in one twenty-five—one as he is, two as they were forty years ago, when the knot was tied, when the knot was tied!
>
> The neighbors will hear and think we've been drinking, and think we've gone swimming in bovine beer, and we three'll know we've been drinking tomato juice—tomato juice!
>
> We're only being rowdy and silly, silly and rowdy, while coming clean, while coming clean!
>
> Somewhere near we had a towel for each, for each a towel—now I'll take mine, you'll take mine, I'll take yours!

It was elfin season. We were frisky and young in the moonlight, splashing and lathering and being lathered, barking and bathing and bathing and barking, and laughing and laughing.

It must have been 1:30 in the morning of a soft October night, a night when wee folk frolic and laugh, and laugh, and laugh on and on.

A Season of Love

More prophetic words I've never spoken than when I told Jeanne in jest that Max might go back to Robinson's barn. He went back again and again, for eight of the next nine days, and each time Jeanne and I, or the two of us together bathed him. There's a saying in Appalachia—I've heard it from Southern Ohio to South Carolina—that when an action is slow or circuitous it's because its doer had to go all the way around Robinson's barn. In another version a lazy or dawdling worker may be castigated as one who has gone all the way around Robinson's barn. In yet another version it comes out as a caution: Now don't you put yourself out, don't you go all the way around Robinson's barn.

All of these sayings touch on Max but one limns his action for what it was. As I said, he went all the way around Robinson's barn on eight days of the next nine. His action was never slow or circuitous, he never lazed or dawdled, and he proved what has always been true: he loves to put himself out. In capsule he is direct and energetic, a born type-A personality, as American and as enterprising as Ben Franklin himself.

Jeanne and I began to understand his strange and compulsive attitude towards Robinson's barn the morning after he got his first tomato juice cleansing. One moment he stood very attentive on the patio, looking like a bright and shiny black gum leaf in the October sunlight; the next moment he had whirled and headed toward Robinson's barn. And he had departed—dashed off—without touching his breakfast, the beginning of a fast that in itself is a live giveaway to those who know the ways of canine males.

Acting on my instinct and Jeanne's infallible intuition I caught up with him two streets away at the Colburn house. He wore an amulet of cow fragrance the way a young man sports a touch of his father's cologne or aftershave, a dash of his father's hair tonic. When I spotted Max near the Colburn garage I whistled and he came zesting toward me, red-tongued and shiny eyed, inviting me to look to the open door of the garage he had just departed. I followed his pointing, but saw only the open door. I reached down and massaged his ear, it was the one spot fragrance free. He turned and barked toward the garage, a summons and an introduction all in one.

There stepped into the morning sun Carolina Belle. Renee Corbett had been right as usual. Carolina Belle was a large coal-black Great Dane, in every line a blueblood, a registered dog that would, if bred to her registered kind, produce a litter of great value. She cast one glance at me, then fixed her eyes on Max. She spoke and he spoke, a soft two-note set of sounds similar yet different from those Max used with Jeanne and me when he arrived to find us still abed after he had had a morning outing. Now she turned and ran towards us, as playful as a kitten, stepping and stopping, dipping her great slender body on her front feet, gathering herself in a rolling movement, approaching but not approaching, then whirling in a circle. Despite her size she was beautiful and coquettish, as graceful as a dragonfly rising and dipping above an August pond.

Max went calling at the Colburn house, Carrie Belle's home, again the next morning, went roundabout by way of Robinson's barn, as I discovered when I retrieved him. By this time word has gone out in the neighborhood, nature has communications that would have shamed Ma Bell at her monopolistic best: Carrie Belle was coming in heat. Present that day was Max, nearest the closed garage door; and Ben and Bert, the Labradors that had somehow found a way through, under, or over their dog-proof fence; a springer spaniel male I did not recognize and a young Irish setter belonging to a woman colleague at Denison.

As I say, Max stood nearest the garage door. I saw no signs of Carrie Belle, and the garage door was down, but Max gave her every indication he knew exactly where she was beyond it. I attached his leash to escort him away. He held fast to the bit of turf he had established till his breath was rasping—you obviously didn't get to be top dog in this competition without a struggle. I took his chain off choke, gentled him by hand, spoke sternly to him, and he permitted himself to be led away although not without snarling at Ben and Bert who themselves began a snapping dispute as to which one should take Max's station nearest the door.

The next morning Max again ignored his breakfast; and he had eaten not one bite of dinner the night before. Fasting was as much a part of this rite as was going roundabout by way of Robinson's barn, and judging by ultimate outcome those human males who suffer infertility may wish to try fasting to test whether limiting the normal digestive processes may not strengthen and speed on their way their dilatory gene-bearing swimmers.

This time the collection of dogs—all males, of course—at or near the Colburn house was astounding. Astounding in numbers, astounding in variety. Ben and Bert had disappeared, probably held under lock and chain in the Pauling basement, since I saw their pen was empty as I passed it. They were not missed, their breed was well represented by three Labradors, two blacks and one buff, the buff a neighborhood veteran who suffered so from arthritis that he sometimes took most of the morning making it to his mailbox and back, but he was there. Well back in the pack too was an ancient malamute of our neighborhood named Ivan—these I recognized as I moved among them to lead Max from the garages door and his twenty feet of turf. I again had trouble getting Max to relinquish battleground won at such cost, but he finally did, not however without voicing his I'll-reckon-with-you-later to the Labradors and an Irish setter and an airedale. As we departed the scene Max even gave a rolling-away-of-thunder growl at those who stood at the very end of the barking order. Across the road in a nearby wood they waited: two wistful beagles, a doleful cocker. They struck me as rank outsiders, probably not even Granville Township dogs, who had come by just in case.

The next day, Friday, October 12, Max did not get an opportunity to go around Robinson's barn or to it. He did go hungry, but that was by his choice, not ours. Jeanne and I had discussed the matter and we had determined that under no circumstances were we to be responsible for Carrie Belle's not being bred to a registered Great Dane that would sire a registerable litter of pups. At the time we also expressed our amazement that the Colburns appeared to make such a slight effort to control Carrie Belle or her suitors. In any event, I walked Max on his leash in the morning. I gave him a lengthy walk to the campus and back—away from the Colburn establishment—deliberately choosing to go upwind of it, being sensitive to Max's keen sense of smell and not wishing to pile anguish on hurt. Because his fasting continued, Max had little need of such a walk. I just wanted him to be comfortable and reconciled to our decision. He seemed so when I returned him to the patio and anchored him by his double-length chain to the maple tree. "This is one day," I informed Jeanne, "Max will not go to Carrie Belle's house."

And again I was prophetic without being right, for as usual I had underestimated Max. Max did not need to go to Carrie Belle's house, Carrie Belle came to his.

The Scotch poet Robert Burns hardly qualified as a theologian; few poets do. But I think he was speaking in tongues when he wrote: "The best laid schemes 'o mice an' men gang aft a-gley," which freely translates "go often awry." My father, much more conversant with God's word and ways than either Burns or I, was fond of quoting this aphorism: "Man proposes, God disposes." Whichever axiom one prefers, the proof occurred on our West Burg Street patio on Friday morning, October 12.

Jeanne and I, as I said, had decreed Max should not be among the canine gallants lined up in hierarchical order before the Colburn garages that day. In the main we did this to guard against Max's mating with Carrie Belle. In part we did it because in bathing Max the might before we had discovered his bruised chest, long since presumed to be completely healed, had developed a tenderness, a sensitivity no doubt caused when he fought his way to the front of that pack of dogs gathered at the Colburn garage. Somehow in jockeying for position or defending his turf he had re-injured his chest, generating such tenderness that he winced or groaned when Jeanne or I touched it in bathing and drying him.

I had been most careful of Max's chest during his morning walk to the campus and back, careful not to have the leash fall under his body to put pressure on his chest. In anchoring him to the maple tree I had been equally careful. As I left for school Max moved to nose my hand goodbye and in doing so stepped across the chain drawing it against his chest. The momentary pressure on the chain caused him to wince and fall back.

"You've got a semi-invalid on your hands, take care," I said to Jeanne who`was busying herself doing up the breakfast dishes.

"I've got a morning's plenty of pear canning to do," she replied. "As soon as I can get to it."

I explain these circumstances because the account that follows is Jeanne's, not mine. I was at school, she was the one human witness on the scene, the one guarding the home hearth, the one thinking pears and doing the pear canning. Here is her account:

"I was working away in the light of the kitchen window paring pears, and it is such a mindless but fun task that I was really running over the whole pear sequence in my mind: Duchess tree bought 1949, thriving, prolific beyond description; the crop, six to twelve bushels of pears each year, in all, hundreds of bushels from one tree. Pear picking at green-ripe stage, when the pear weight, lifted against the stem, causes the stem to let go, to speak for the pear itself, to say, 'I'm green-ripe, take me.' Held as these green-ripe pears have been, held two weeks out of the sun at room temperature they achieve perfect texture and flavor, and the smooth Duchess flesh spills juicy goodness.

"Then before you could say 'Robinson's barn' I had the pears pared and halved ready to preserve, was adding them to the sugared water, setting them to boil; I had the quart mason jars scalding, to be sterile, and I was thinking all this is humdrum fun but necessary. In October I am tempering and sweetening January and February. That's when I became aware Max was standing at the end of his chain looking past the grape arbor to the pine woods. What alerted me was the peculiar tone of his bark: 'Hey man, what gives! Jolly Jesu, who'd believe it!'

"And from the shadows of the pine woods, a matching bark, higher, and if I must say so, feminine. Then this marvelous female—a real duchess—stepping from the shadows, trailed by four clowns: two Labradors, one black, one buff, and a young Irish setter, over his depth; and, well to the rear, ancient Ivan. One of the Labradors, the black, came too close, made as if to head off the duchess—she was Carrie Belle, of course—and she grabbed him by the ruff, threw him to the ground. And walked on, unperturbed, beautiful. She turned sideways at the grape arbor and snarled at the buff Labrador. He and the Irish setter retreated, joined the black Labrador who had slunk to the shadows of the pines, where Ivan had stopped.

"She came on and Max leaned to the end of his chain. He said something, sort of a two-note song. She replied. She sang this way: 'You—me, you—me, you—me?' She came on, they touched noses, and Max was prancing sideways against his chain. She came closer, eyed the chain, sniffed at it, as if to say, 'It's there, we'll reckon with it.'

Max glanced toward me in the window, as if he were saying, 'This isn't cricket, can't you do something, Momma? Don't you see my problem?'

"That's when the truth hit me: That Carrie Belle is here to be mated. That's when I shouted out the window. And then I'm sure she saw me for the first time, she had had her eyes so fixed on Max. I shouted: 'You go home! You go home!'

My shout surprised her. She drew back and retreated to the grape arbor, faded into the camouflage of its shadow, and glared at me. That's when I exclaimed 'Oh dear' and ran to the telephone. I called the Colburn number—took a minute to find it—and got no answer. I thought 'Oh dear,' and ran back to the kitchen. I had to adjust the flame under the pears, they were boiling over, and when I looked out the window, there she was standing beside Max, well within the limits of his chain, and he was trying to mount her—from the side.

"I thought 'Oh dear' and turned the gas out under the pears for fear they'd overcook. And I went out on the patio and shouted 'You go home! Carrie Belle, you go home!' She didn't budge. She just looked at me as if to say, 'What's eating you?' Then she turned a trifle and Max was trying to mount her properly, but of course she stands half a foot higher being a Great Dane, and I thought, 'Thank you, Lord, for making those two dogs of different sizes.' Maybe I said it, for suddenly it dawned on me, they just couldn't do it.

"That's when I turned on the fire under the pears, having tried one with the fork and found it half-cooked.

"When I looked again, she was climbing the bank beside the fireplace, thinking that the difference in height had to be changed, a situation that made poor Maxie even more disadvantaged, and I thought, 'Thank you, Lord.' Maxie was jumping trying to mount her, and when he fell down he yipped in pain, and I thought how sorry I was for him.

"Just then the pears boiled over for the second time. I turned the fire down and glanced out the window. Carrie Belle and Maxie had moved farther along the bank, but she was still standing above him and he was struggling just to keep his footing. I took time then to draw out the sterilized jars and to fill them—to can the pears, nine quarts in all. And the self-sealing jars all sealed themselves, which doesn't always happen. That took at least fifteen minutes, and when I looked out the window I could see where Carrie Belle and Max had tramped the myrtle on the bank flat, but had come no closer to succeeding. Again I thought, 'Thank you, Lord.'

"That's when I went to call the Colburns a second time—I thought of calling you but knew you'd be in your two hour seminar. It took me less time to call the Colburns this time, having the number, but again I got no response.

"When next I looked out the window I felt real sorry for the two of them. They had both tried so hard to do what comes natural. That's when I began to feel sort of ambivalent about our prohibition. But I didn't have to do anything, for as I watched Carrie Belle leaned close to Max on the bank and the sang their little two-note song head to head. Then Carrie Belle stepped down on the level patio and stretched her front feet far out on the grass, kneeling so she left her rump at just Max's height, and before I could say or do a thing they were one. He was doing it, and doing it, and he was bumping his bruised chest and yipping, and asking: 'How can anything so painful feel so good?'"

Jeanne related that account when I got home from school on Friday, October 12. At that first telling I thought to ask what she did next. She said, "I did the only decent thing—when I saw they were married and I knew Max was soon going to be dragged around in reverse, I went out and unsnapped his chain. What would you have done, may I ask?"

"I'd have done exactly what you did, dear."

It was later that night when I asked Jeanne one further question, and I record it here just to finish off this wedding episode. I asked, "What do you suppose was the verb that went with that little two-note song Carrie Belle and Max sang—how did it go?"

"You—me, you—me, you—me?"

"Yes, what verb would go with that question?"

Jeanne grew reflective. "You know I wondered about that. How about *need* or *want*? What do you think the verb might be?"

"Those two are fine," I said. "Both are good serviceable four letter words, the kind we often overlook."

The Honeymoon

Max and Carrie Belle's honeymoon continued through the long weekend and well into the following week. Just when it ended neither Jeanne nor I know. We do know it took Max to Robinson's barn each day for another four days; we gave him four evening baths before we convinced him the fragrance of cow manure wasn't what Carrie Belle really found attractive. Actually, I think Carrie Belle herself may have let him know enough was enough, and she much preferred that he come directly to her house without bothering to go clear around Robinson's barn before they could set off on their daily run.

Those runs, by a long-legged couple as fleet as shadows, were marvels to behold. The only comparable sight I can recall had occurred the summer Jeanne and I built our house with a view of what was then open countryside where the white pines now flourished. One morning in June I had seen a red fox running the ridge of Johnson grass—floating along as if propelled by his tail, his nippy feet being set down like a pianist's fingers, as he moved toward me. At the last minute he had caught my scent and had turned to join up with his mate running a parallel course thirty yards to his right. He had joined her and they had teamed off together, shoulder to shoulder, their buoyant white-tipped tails like jets propelling them through the brown grass.

Daily Max and Carrie Belle coursed through the pine woods to a splendid stand of ancient beeches left over from those halcyon days when passenger pigeons by the millions toured the Ohio countryside, beech grove to beech grove, darkening the sun in their passing as they foraged the mast of those silvery giants. One has to have had the run of a primeval beech wood throughout the fall of an Indian summer, has to have played hide and seek and chase and catch among those silvery trunks under a cornflower blue sky, has to have thrown his or herself, pleasurably tired, upon that bed of leathery-feathery shining beech leaves to have even the remotest notion of the honeymoon of Max and Carrie Belle. Jeanne and I had a good notion, and our knowledge and countenancing of their pleasure may well have offended some envious deity or nymph of forest or grove. I'm sure we encouraged Max's inclination to excess, for other than bathing him after each of his Robinson barn capers, we left him on his own. After all, we reasoned, honeymooners deserve their privacy.

Max did not return home on Thursday night. Jeanne and I joked about it at breakfast, and she said she'd walk over to the Colburn house and pick him up after I left for school. She called me later in the morning to say she had gone to the Colburn's and had not found Max; she had seen Carrie Belle out on her morning run but there was no sign of Max. I told Jeanne he might possibly have stayed overnight somewhere on campus—I was remembering Polly Edwards as though she were still in school doing all night phone duty at Shaw Hall, as if I might hear her warm voice on the phone. I told Jeanne I'd keep an eye out for Max on the quad. I did, and I checked in with Molly Murphy in Slayter's Snack Bar; she had not seen Max for ten days or two weeks. I did not find Max on campus on Friday, and he did not show up Friday night. I got up three or four times during the night thinking I had heard him announcing himself at the back door. Either I was dreaming or it was the wind's moaning, for Max was not at the back door singing his little two-note song softly so as not to disturb Jeanne; he was not there with his bright shiny face saying, "Hey Poppa, let me in. Your prodigal son is home."

Saturday morning Jeanne and I took stock of the situation. Never had Max been gone for more than one night; never since Charles and Bill had packed off to college had the emptiness of our house been more pervasive. I tried to console Jeanne, tried to be more optimistic than I was. "He's got his name tag and his license. When someone picks him up, they'll give us a call. It's just a matter of time."

After breakfast Jeanne gathered the few pictures we had of Max, none current, and asked me to pump up the tires on her bicycle. "I'll just ride out Burg and around Louden Street and make a few inquiries, maybe swing down around New Burg," she said, her voice breaking.

I picked up Max's leash and said, "I'll take a hike down through the pine woods, through the beech woods, just in case he's camping out someplace."

"You want me to go over to the Colburn's again?" Jeanne asked. "I could start there."

"Why not," I said. I added: "I'll circle around

Robinson's barn from the beech woods, that way we'll cover all the runs."

We made our rounds and found no sign, no one who had seen Max or so much as heard the jingle of his tags. Saturday afternoon we got in the car and drove to the campus. We traveled every road, passed every dorm, every classroom, every sorority and fraternity house, the Field House, all the playing fields and tennis courts—drove at snail's pace with both windows down, so that my whistle could be heard as far as possible. No luck. We returned and ate a sandwich and began casing Granville in the same systematic way; we worked as far east as Cherry Valley Road, as far south as The Evergreens Restaurant and the IGA lot, as far north as Cherry Ridge and the Denison Biological Reserve. Nothing.

Saturday night I again awakened three or four times and each time went to the front door and to the back. I had imagined—or had I dreamed—I heard Max barking. I had an eerie feeling he was being held and was barking, barking, calling for Jeanne and me, but where? Where?

Sunday morning Jeanne said to me, "It's three days—three days! He could have traveled fifty miles in three days."

"Five hundred, a thousand miles in someone's car," I said. "You don't suppose that Granville patrolman was cluing me on something when he suggested Max might be stolen—that it was a heaven-sent warning I should have heard and heeded."

"I doubt that God would employ a Granville patrolman as a messenger," Jeanne said. She saw the look on my face and said, "Forgive me, PB. I've been thinking equally despondent thoughts." She raised her hand to her mouth. "We haven't checked with the police."

"They'd have called. He has his name tag and his license and besides they know him. They'd have called."

Sunday morning I went to the office to catch up on correspondence and write out half a dozen recommendations for seniors and recent graduates applying to various graduate programs. I handled the letters and recommendations, and then walked down the front drag, as the steep main road to "Fair Denison on the hill" is called. Max often went with me on that walk to pick up the Sunday New York *Times*; he always turned the walk into an outing. I discovered now the hill was longer both ways than I had remembered, the uphill climb became a real bummer. While getting the *Times* at Taylor's I had seen the patrolman out front and had asked if he had seen Max. He hadn't, but he said he remembered Max very well. He was kind and concerned, and said he'd keep an eye out and call us at once if he saw Max anywhere on his rounds.

Jeanne and I were desperate now, and Monday after class I called the Licking County Dog Pound from my office. The phone rang and rang and finally a man who identified himself as Raymond Hawser answered, accompanied by a tumult of barking dogs. "Here, " Raymond Hawser said, "let me shut that door." I heard a door close and the brazen barking receded slightly but remained as background to our conversation. I identified myself and explained that we had lost our dog, a male of mixed breed, black and tan, short-haired, weighing about seventy-five pounds, who answered to the name of Max. I added that he was wearing an identification tag with our phone number and street address and he was wearing his Licking County License #1071.

"When did you lose him?"

"Thursday of last week."

"We'd have called you within twenty-four hours if he was wearing a tag."

"He had on both a name tag with our phone number and a valid license," I said.

"A tag is a license, that's what I mean," Raymond Hawser said. "We have a list of all licensed dogs, and we try to call within three or four hours, always within twenty-four hours."

"You wouldn't—mightn't have put him to sleep—disposed of him?" I said.

"We do our disposing on Tuesdays and Fridays, and then only on dogs that have been here four days. Like I said we'd have called you immediately if we'd picked up your tagged dog. We get no pleasure doing in dogs or cats but we have only so many pens, so much budget for food and care."

"I'm sure of that," I said.

"I should just tell you," Raymond Hawser went on, "Any untagged dog becomes the property of the Pound if kept for seventy-two hours. And then he can be claimed by anyone who's willing to pay the $5 pick-up fee and $5 license fee. If the dog is licensed we charge $6 pick-up fee plus the board of $1.50 per day for however long he's been held."

"I'd sure be happy to pay those fees for Max," I said. There was silence except for the background barking.

"Well thank you, Mr. Hawser, for talking with me." I hung up.

At dinner that evening Jeanne told me she had again biked the rounds of the neighborhood and done every street in town as far as the bypass highway, without results. I told her I had called the Pound in Newark to the same effect. I then rehearsed the conversation I had had with Mr. Hawser, including the barking dogs as backup.

Monday evening we waited—and when the phone rang we each leaped to answer. I took the call; it was a woman asking us if we wanted to take advantage of an Olan Mills photograph special. We had a second call; it was a man calling long distance from Columbus who started out by asking if we owned our own home and if we did, did we have storm doors and windows against the coming winter.

"Winter's already here," I said as I slammed the phone in place.

"PB," Jeanne said.

"I know," I said.

But I didn't really know—does anyone ever really know by what slight threads hang the lives of those we love? How little I knew I discovered the next morning, Tuesday, when I came out of my 9:30-10:30 class to find the phone ringing. It was Jeanne.

"PB, I've got some terrible news," she said. She was trying to control her voice. "Renee Corbett stopped here at the door not five minutes ago. She missed her morning bus and stayed home and was riding her bike to school When I answered the door she said: 'Ms. B., do you know what? I just found these on the side of the road in front of the Pauling's house. I knew you had been looking for Max and I came down to give them to you. Maybe Ben and Bert were fighting with Max and pulled them off.'" Jeanne's voice broke. "She held out Max's name tag and license."

"I don't see—" I began.

"The Pound," Jeanne said. "If by any chance they picked Max up on Thursday he wouldn't have been wearing his name tag, his license—"

"Oh my god," I said. "You hang up!"

I was dialing to get 93, the outside line, then the Pound: 323-0247.

"Licking County Dog Pound, Vicky Hauptman speaking." The distant barking accompanying her voice told me the office door was shut.

"Miss Hauptman," I said, "could I please speak to Raymond Hawser, it's urgent."

"He's busy. This is the morning we dispose of dogs and he's—"

"I desperately need to speak to him," I said. "He'll understand."

"You call back in half and hour or forty-five minutes and he'll be available—"

"Please don't hang up," I said. "Listen, I'll tell you: it's just possible you might have—I'm not sure—but you might have our dog Max, you might have picked him up, and if you picked him up last Thursday—"

"If that's the case I think it's too late, You see, the pens are full and—"

"Please. If Raymond Hawser could just come to the phone—"

"Hang on!"

The barking of dogs told me the office door had opened—remained open. A minute later a voice:

"Raymond Hawser speaking." The tone said, "Now

what!"

"Mr. Hawser," I said. "I'm the guy who called you yesterday and—" In three sentences I gave him the story of the tags and repeated Max's description.

He said, "We've got five or six black and brown mongrel males to match your description." He stopped and I heard him ask: "Are they still alive? Pen twelve—or is it thirteen?" Then he said, "I'm sorry but—"

"If you could just wait till I drove over," I said. "I can be there in fifteen minutes. If you could just wait I'd be glad to pay you to keep all five of them."

"We don't do that," he said. "If we had some sure way of knowing if one was your dog, we'd keep him—and I'd be stretching it to do that."

Like a light it hit me: Of course, of course, someone somewhere knew this, that's why Max was given his wound, his mark. "Mr. Hawser," I said. "Max has a notch on his tongue, if you'd just look at his tongue it's notched on the left side where he got it cut almost half across when a pup. You'll see it if you look for it. Could you please look?"

"Man, you can't look at a dog's tongue unless the dog is dead. And to peer in five dog's mouths? I'm sorry." I sensed Raymond Hawser's hand easing the phone towards the cradle and I was powerless to stop it. Then I heard a woman's voice—Vicky Hauptman's flat-midwestern voice—from a distance like a bell:

"I think I know the one, Raymond. I saw it when Ralph brought them in on Thursday. He'd been running hard and his tongue hung out a mile. I'll show you."

"Just a minute, " Raymond Hawser said, "Vicky here

says she might be able to identify the dog, and if she can we'll hold him."

"You do that, you do that," I said. "Look at his notched tongue. Speak to him , his name is Max. I'll be there in fifteen minutes. Thank you. Hug Vicky for me."

"Don't you go breaking the speed law or your damn fool neck," Raymond Hawser growled. His voice seemed to complement the barking din, and he was muttering several things about me as I hung up and took the steps of Fellows Hall three at a time going down, the steps Wolfgang and Max had climbed with such glee in other years.

A Legacy

That December in Ohio was as warm and gentle as December, 1977, had been cold and tempestuous. The average daily temperature for the month was 6 degrees above normal, and during one week or ten days in the middle of the month new record highs were set almost daily throughout the state. Whether sun and moon and the entire planetary train, with sea and jet stream and air mass, formed some beneficial conspiracy of excess I don't know. I do know that it was a time of unexpected occurrences and behaviors, which bore all the earmarks of springtime delirium.

As luck had it I gave a final examination during that period of natural perturbation, and not only did I have reason to keep the windows fully open throughout the two hour test but I later discovered that several otherwise reliable students turned in papers that answered too many questions and two students failed to reckon with half of the questions. As I was carrying these December final examination blue books to the station wagon—blue books still to be graded—I saw a dozen or fifteen men and women students, white and black, skipping and frolicking *barefoot* on the quad between the Union and Fellows Hall.

Friday, December 14, Carrie Belle Colburn gave birth to her litter. Jeanne and I and Max heard of the happening the next day. We were taking a Saturday morning stroll out Burg Street—Jeanne coatless, I in shirt sleeves, Max in his year-around—when we were overtaken by Renee Corbett on her red bicycle. She came to a tire-squealing stop that brought us to a halt; she stood straddling her bicycle as she spoke: "Mr. and Mrs. B., do you and Max know what happened to Carrie Belle Colburn last night?"

I looked at Jeanne, we both looked at Max.

"She had twelve pups! I saw them, I counted them. They're all black. Their eyes are shut and they couldn't see me but I got to watch them as Carrie Belle fed them. She's a good mother."

"Twelve pups!" I exclaimed. "Carrie Belle had a dozen pups." I looked at Max who lifted his chin full profile and peered into the distance as if the future lay that way.

"I'll bet Carrie Belle will be a good mother," Jeanne said. "She looked it."

"The Colburns," Renee Corbett said, "aren't real sure but they think the father was a Labrador, maybe Ben or Bert. I wish I knew for sure. I'm going to tell this at 'Share and Tell' on Monday, and I'd like to have it right."

"Of course you would," Jeanne said. She looked at me. I looked to Max who had turned and was looking in the direction of the Colburn house.

"I can say the Colburns *believe* the father is a Labrador."

"That's fair enough," I said. "Twelve pups!"

"I just thought you'd like to know." Renee Corbett stood on her pedal and moved ahead, picked up speed.

Jeanne and I looked at each other. Her eyes held me at point.

"Well you can't be absolutely sure," I said.

"I am *sure* sure," Jeanne said. She looked at Max. "What do you think, Maxie?"

Max was watching Renee sail down the road but he turned at the sound of his name and tilted his head to peer at Jeanne. She repeated her question. He responded with a reverse tilt of his head, a movement that enunciated a line repeated from an inaugural address: "You ain't seen nothing yet." He looked at me: "Let's get on with this stroll."

"There's something special about this father business," I said to Jeanne. "How did Freud put it, the most important day in the life of any man is the day of the death of his father. Presumably he meant that's the day a man stands on his own feet—has to be himself, his own person."

Jeanne said: "Then you'd have to know the father *to have* that important day." Her tone carried reservations on Freud and his pronouncements.

"Maybe," I said, "but if you don't know the father the death has already occurred—"

"Or might occur at some date unspecified, unknown."

"The not-knowing is the death," I said. "Look at Max here for your proof. Could he be what he has been, what he is, if he'd had to live in the shadow of his father?"

Jeanne remained to be convinced. "I know—and you know—he is *the father* of Carrie Belle's twelve pups. And the question is, are you going to so inform the Colburns?"

"One doesn't just go up to complete strangers—" I began. "Twelve," I added, "that number does sound Maxish."

"And what about that promise you made that wonderful Black girl—you said if Max ever sired a litter you'd get her one."

"Polly Edwards," I said. "She's gone off to Yale Divinity School and could hardly care for a pup in New Haven. We'll just have to see."

"A promise is a promise," Jeanne said.

"I'd sure like to—" I said. We were moving along, Max pulling Jeanne, Jeanne pulling me.

Any uncertainty about Max's being the father—was it ever in doubt?—was dispelled on Sunday morning when Max and I met Renee Corbett outside Taylor's Drug Store where we'd gone to pick up the Sunday New York *Times.* Clad in a red velvet dress and white sweater, sporting black sandals and red knee socks, Renee danced over to stand with her hand on Max's dome-shaped head as she proclaimed:

"Mr. B., do you know what Carrie Belle did yesterday?"

"She didn't hurt the pups?"

"Oh no. She loves them. she had one more. That makes thirteen. I saw it, not when it was born but right after when it was with the others. It's just like them, except it has a different birthday. Now I'll have that to tell. I may have to ask for somebody else's turn at 'Share and Tell' tomorrow."

"That is fabulous!" I said as much to myself as to Renee. "That is fantastic. That last pup—number thirteen—was born on December 15. That's Max's birthday and now it's the thirteenth pup's birthday. Do you hear that, Max?"

At home with Jeanne I became more demonstrative. Engaging in a Renee Corbett dance, I inquired: "Mrs. B., do you want to know—Carrie Belle had another pup."

"That's a baker's dozen!" Jeanne exclaimed. She turned and asked Max a question I couldn't hear.

"That's the final Maxish touch," I said. "The proverbial last straw."

"It's both those things, and more," Jeanne said. "It had better be the last pup—poor Carrie Belle." She turned to Max and repeated what seemed to be her earlier question.

"What did you just ask him?"

"I asked him, 'Are you happy with your present—presents—Birthday Boy?'"

Max, as he often did when addressed directly by Jeanne or me, twisted his head to one side and listened intently. This time he shook out his umbrella ears and elevated his dome-shaped head: "So what? Nothing to it. Glory be! So be it!"

Max's taking in stride his fathering thirteen pups in one mating worked on my conscience and gave me reason to follow up on my promise to give Polly Edwards a pup, should Max sire a litter. After all, with thirteen pups on their hands the Colburns would surely be willing to part with one. Then too, Jeanne endorsed my conscience with a gentle reminder morning and evening that I had made a promise involving our family, and Max had done his part manfully.

From the college alumni office I secured Polly Edwards' New Haven, Connecticut address and phone number and called her on a Friday evening. I inquired about her divinity school studies—par for the Christian ministry in a lip-service world, she said—and told her of my latest doings and Max's, and asked if she could use a Max-fathered pup, the said little Max or Maxine mothered by a Great Dane.

"Strange that you'd call me about a pup," she replied in her warm drawl, "for I just yesterday disposed of a stray tiger cat I'd been housing. Disposed of him by delivering him to 'Animal Haven' as the Humane Society's shelter for strays is called here on campus where we collect more than our number. Anyhow, to quote our late E. E. Cummings, I'm living like those infamous Cambridge ladies: 'in a furnished soul.' And New Haven—Yale's New Haven—has absolutely nothing on Harvard's Cambridge when one is in that condition."

"Then you could really use one of Max's pups?" I said. "I can probably get you the pick of the litter, male or female. They'd be ready in five or six weeks, I imagine"

"Oh no," Polly Edwards said. "I only got rid of my tiger-man to avoid getting kicked out of my digs." She paused. "I'd sure like to have one of Maxie's own, but my days of being free to own a dog, any pet, are down the road a few years. For the foreseeable future I must remain like Cummings' moon that 'rattles like a piece of angry candy in its box of sky, lavender and cornerless.'"

"You and Cummings make the moon and sky beautiful—biblical," I said.

"I love things *au naturel*." Polly Edwards laughed. "Like Max. Do give him a hug for me. Please do, and remind him to mind *his* father." Again she paused. "And tell him I'm delighted he's spreading his genes. This old world's a bit short on love."

"I will," I said.

"He still has all that alertness of a German shepherd, that sweetness of a hound?"

"Even more so," I said. "Here, I'll get him on the phone. Max!"

Max, who had been standing at the back door listening—following—a strange and eerie "yip, yip, yip" that echoed dimly from beyond the patio, heard his name and came to me. I lowered the phone and Polly Edwards spoke to him. Max heard her voice and glanced to my face, then again lowered his head to Polly's cooing.

"Say something to your old friend Polly Edwards," I said. At my urging he sniffed at the phone, but he refused to speak—refused to take part in our palaver. I raised the phone to my mouth. "Only a sniff, a kiss."

"Do give him a hug for me," Polly said.

"Will do, will do," I said. "And you take care, Polly."

"Will do, will do. And you the same," she echoed as I hung up.

"At least you did the right thing by that sweet girl," Jeanne announced from the kitchen doorway where she'd come from tidying up the dinner dishes.

"Give me time enough and I almost always do the right thing."

"You just have to give your father and Ebenezer Scrooge time, Maxie," Jeanne said.

No sooner were Jeanne's words out than Max delivered his pronouncement on me: a long, low reverberating groan.

"And don't you put in your dog-gone comments!" I warned him. "You wouldn't even a say a word on the telephone."

Max, eyes shining, fixed me with stare and blinked, as he often did in shaking off a happy reprimand.

I spoke to Jeanne: "Boy, you two sure know how to pillory the innocent." She smiled as I continued, "I hope you both will be satisfied with my New Year's vow, for you're in it."

"When do we get to do what?" Jeanne asked.

"I promised—now I use a much abused word—I *promised* myself that you and Max and I would march over to the Colburns on New Year's day to meet Carrie Belle's folks, and Carrie Bell's and Max's offspring. Monday—New Year's—being a holiday, the Colburns are almost sure to be home."

"I hope you'll be neighborly enough to call ahead," Jeanne said.

"I hoped you'd do that, " I said. "Since Max won't talk on the telephone."

That my New Year's vow was to be as inconsequential as most New Year's vows we learned early Monday morning when Jeanne and Max and I waltzed out Burg Street on an early Monday morning constitutional. The squint-eyed winter's sun was just clearing the eastern hills when we were overtaken by Renee Corbett who came to a screeching halt before us and stepped down to straddle her bicycle."Mr. and Mr. B., do you and Max know about the Colburns—"

The gist of Renee's first share-and-tell of the New Year was that a giant orange Atlas moving van had roared up narrow Burg Street from the opposite end on Saturday morning. The movers—three burly men—had loaded the goods and chattels of Dr. and Mrs. Alexander Colburn to haul them to Columbia, South Carolina. He was going back to his old company as research director. His goods were traveling south by van, his wife by plane, and he and Carrie Belle and her thirteen nursing pups had set out by station wagon on Sunday morning to drive to South Carolina. Jeanne, Max and I stood stock still—letting the news sink in—even as Renee Corbett, who seemed to grow taller by the hour, stood up on her pedal, pushed off and sped away.

"Well Max," I finally said, "They've shipped your family to the land of cotton."

"Rhymes with *forgotten,*" Jeanne said forlornly.

Max looked from me to Jeanne.

"It'll be all right," I said. "It will be *all right*." To Jeanne I added: "At least we can be damned glad Polly Edwards didn't take me up on that pup offer. I'd be up Promise Creek without a paddle, and we'd all be making a trip to Columbia, South Carolina."

"Think of that trip for poor Dr. Colburn," Jeanne said. "A twelve to fifteen hour drive in a station wagon loaded with Carrie Belle and thirteen two-week-old pups. No wonder he told Renee Corbett: 'I'm not looking forward to this trip.'"

I explained to Max: "That trip would put more than your good genes to the test. If Polly Edwards knew, she'd offer a prayer for dogs and man."

Max understood what I said, for he stood in the road with his head on tilt.

Don Juan

I never expected Max to take seriously my reprimanding him for failing to speak to Polly Edwards. But Max prided himself on his powers to communicate when he needed to, and he proved those powers and gave me my comeuppance in what Jeanne named the sleeping bag incident.

That incident began with a house a mile and a half from ours—at the corner of Elm and Cherry Streets in Granville—that had over the summer undergone extensive remodeling and was now occupied by a new family, a young professional husband and wife named Anders, and a new-to-this-neighborhood black Labrador, name and sex unknown to us. Max, whose senses enabled him to identify strange dogs at distances that would enlighten those who probe the skies for extra-terrestrial life, determined that the black Labrador was indeed a female approaching her season.

So it was that as winter reached its full power and January gave way to February, Max began disappearing after his evening meal. Several nights I found him waiting for his bus near the flagpole outside the Student Union on campus, leading me to assume he was merely making his usual campus rounds. But one evening as he took his departure Jeanne remarked that not only was he disappearing regularly at nightfall, but he had stopped eating, hadn't eaten for two days.

"You know what that means?" she said.

"Not again," I said. "Who and where is she?"

"Who is Sylvia?" Jeanne sang. "What is she, that all our swains commend her?" She added: "I think she may be that black Labrador down at the remodeled house. I saw Max move from one window to the other—testing the air—as we drove by coming from the IGA on Saturday."

"As you drove by," I said. "You mean he's acute enough—?"

"He's cute and acute enough," Jeanne said.

It was snowing the evening Jeanne made that remark. Max had disappeared at nightfall, and I assumed I might be making a slippery late night bus-run to Elm and Cherry. Surprise, surprise! Max showed up promptly at eleven thirty at the close of the late news program. Soaking wet he spoke his little two-note arrival speech at the door, entered smartly, and walked back and forth under a towel, and went to bed.

Except for no snow, the next five nights went on in a similar way. But he was plainly into his female-in-heat fast, and he spoke to be let out the back door soon after nightfall each evening.

Throughout that late February week temperatures had been winter normal for Ohio, rising to around freezing during the day and falling into the teens or single digits at night. But then came a Friday when an Alberta Clipper moved through, the sky cleared, the moon shone, and the red alcohol in our outside thermometer sought its deep-red pool. By nine o'clock that evening it was zero, by ten it was six below and falling, and by eleven it was ten below and still falling. I listened to the eleven o'clock news—heard it through to its sporty close—but no sound of Max. I opened the door and felt the wind—it was blowing at near gale force, or so my Navy experience told me. Still there as no sign of Max. I settled down with a book—Fawn Brodie's *Thomas Jefferson*—that a poet friend had given me and that I'd been meaning to read for years. I read a chapter, another, another. When I next looked at the clock it was 2 a.m., and I was halfway through Thomas Jefferson's great troubled life. I stepped to the patio and checked the thermometer: 17 below zero. I put the book aside and consulted Jeanne who had been long asleep.

When Jeanne was stirring, she murmured: "Is that the wind I hear?" she sat upright, pulling the coverlet around her neck. "How cold is it?"

"Seventeen below by the thermometer. With that wind the chill factor could be pushing forty or more."

"More," she said morosely. "You'll have to go get him."

"I warned him I wasn't coming after him."

"We both warned him," she said. "But if he lies there on the ground all night he'll be frozen to death by morning."

"I hoped you'd say that," I said. "If I can get the car started I'm on my way." I was pulling on my fur hat, reaching for my storm coat and fur-lined gloves.

Luck was with me. The old engine turned over and in no time I was out the driveway, tooling down deserted Burg Street in fierce wind and moonlight so bright I hardly needed headlights. As I turned right at the stoplight on Broadway and

Cherry, the stoplight itself was dancing like a body on a gallows' rope. I looked—peered—ahead to the remodeled house at Cherry and Elm, expecting to see the familiar black body in the yard. No sign of it. I slowed and turned onto Elm Street. No sign of Max, who by this time should have heard his familiar bus motor and be coming toward me.

My worst fears took a quantum leap when I saw a dark object in the moonlight. A frozen body? No, it looked more like a rolled up rug. No—my god—a sleeping bag! I swung to the curb, left the motor in neutral, and walked toward the sleeping bag. As I got within five or six steps to it, up came a familiar head decorated with umbrella ears, Max in silhouette.

"Max! Max, you scoundrel!" I whispered, squatting beside him. "Where the devil did you get that sleeping bag?"

He crawled clear of the bag, stretched, and then as if feeling the cold for the first time, wagged his tail, touched my nose with his, and dashed off briskly to the purring station wagon.

Jeanne must have heard us enter the house, for she called sleepily: "Did you find him?"

"Yep."

"Where was he? I'll bet he's frozen stiff."

"Bet again. He's not cold at all. I'm colder than he is—"

"Where was he?"

"He was lying just outside the door of the Labrador's house in a sleeping bag, as cozy as could be. When he crawled out he stretched and looked at me to ask what the devil was I doing out in such foul weather."

Max had gone off to his water bowl to indulge in a long tongue-slurping drink. Now he rushed to the bedroom, feet prancing, eyes glowing.

"A sleeping bag?" Jeanne muttered. "Now you are cutting it out of whole cloth."

"You ask him, just ask him," I said.

Jeanne flipped the cover over her head. She would not be baited by prevarication at 3 a.m. even when practiced by man and dog.

Saturday morning breakfast: although he was not touching food himself, Max bustled about the kitchen overseeing Jeanne and me as we downed hot cereal and juice and coffee. Jeanne was in a questioning mood, and she finally spoke her mind: "Did you do that night stuff again—tell me Max was in a sleeping bag at the Labrador's house or did I just dream it?"

"I told you the truth, Sister. As soon as you finish your breakfast we're getting in that old buggy and driving straight to the corner of Elm and Cherry."

Jeanne said: "You can bet your shorts we are, Brother. This time I'm calling your hand without moonlight for you to Irish in."

We made the quick trip to the corner of Elm and Cherry. As we turned the corner onto Elm, the morning sun lighting our way, we saw it. Like a large Christmas ornament: a green canvas sleeping bag flashing a red plaid lining—hanging not in an evergreen but in a small leafless maple. Evidently someone had hung the bag to air it.

"Well I'll be—" Jeanne began.

"You'll be dog-goned—just as I was," I said. "So, has Max made you a believer in your husband?"

"Max!" Jeanne turned to the glowing brown eyes, the

ebony nose resting at her elbow, "How could you pull that off?"

How Max conned his way into a sleeping bag we learned a couple weeks later when we met Mrs. Anders and her Labrador—the name was Susie, not Sylvia, we discovered—on the street near Fuller's Market. I apologized to Mrs. Anders, explaining that Max, who was across the street snoozing in the back of his bus, had been the black and tan hound that plagued them during the cold snap when Susie was in heat.

"He caused us no problem," Mrs. Anders said. "He did send a couple neighbors' dogs packing."

"Uh—" I glanced at Jeanne, "did you folks by any chance put out a sleeping bag for Max?"

"Lorenz did that. He said he couldn't just let that nice hound lie out there—-so gentle, so persistent, so loyal—and freeze to death. So he took out one of his old mountain climbing sleeping bags and your hound crawled right in. When Lorenz came back in the house he said he hadn't felt so good since the night he won his Eagle Scout badge."

"You thank him for Jeanne and me," I said.

"And Max," Jeanne said. "For the three of us."

Fatal Attractions

If the sleeping bag incident was an immediate and happy link to the Polly Edwards' call, later there came a sad and tragic link. It hinged on the eerie, high-pitched "yip-yip-yip" that captured Max's attention and held him spellbound while I was on the telephone. The yip-yip-yip belonged to one of his canine kind—ghostly, blond, female. Rail thin and as elusive as a moonbeam, she tongued her siren's call across our hillside and throughout the depths of Robinson's beech woods for three years. Whose dog she was—if anybody's—and what her breeding I never did discover.

A friend who knew dogs and saw her close-up in daylight—Dr. Betsy Arnold of Denison University's Biology Department, a national authority on coyotes and all Canidae—theorized that the yip-yip-yipping female could have sprung from an Eskimo Spitz crossed with coyote. Whatever her lineage and bloodline, her strange bark mesmerized Max for the better part of three years. And even after her swift feet carried her to parts unknown, her strange bark lingered so that Max and Jeanne and I heard it as the death knell it became.

I saw "Circe"—as Jeanne named her—up close only once, and that was on a foggy night in early May, 1989, when her yip-yip-yip echoed at the very edge of our patio. While I stood fixed in place—trying my best to discern where fog left off and white fur began—she exchanged momentary tail-wagging, nose-touching greetings with Max. What she whispered during that brief exchange I don't know, but whatever it was it added him to the pack of eight or ten males who dashed after her, up hill and down dale, when she came in heat that fall.

And if ever a female sprang a steel trap on a lustful but loving male, Circe sprang such a trap on Max. It came about this way: Denison University, during a previous summer, had completely renovated its ancient football stadium, converting the woods-bordered site into a football-track-and-field facility of Olympic dimensions. As part of the renovation the college had installed an ornate entryway to the sports complex, an entryway with turnstile and fence of eight-foot high wrought iron spikes. The space between the steel spikes measured exactly five inches—small enough to keep out all human beings, but of exactly the right dimension to permit Circe to pass through and to catch madly pursuing Max between chest and haunches.

Max had responded to Circe's siren yip-yip-yip on a Tuesday evening during the last week of November. I casually looked for him and inquired about him on campus on Wednesday. No sightings, no word. That evening I had a call from Josh Pursey of the Denison History Department. He had seen Max, along with a pack of males disappearing into the ravined woods that separates the academic quad from the athletic fields. Thursday afternoon Betsy Arnold called to tell me she had seen Max running with a pack of dogs led by that strange female whose likely Eskimo Spitz-coyote parentage we had discussed.

"Where did you see him?" I asked.

"On the far side of Lake Hudson," Betsy Arnold said.

"Way out there? You're sure it was Max? He was seen on campus last evening."

"Oh, it was Max all right," Betsy Arnold said. "And I'd know that female anywhere, the one your Jeanne named Circe. I keep an eye out for her, for I have the feeling she'll end up in my coyote skull collection someday."

"Thanks, Betsy," I said. "Since the legendary Circe took Odysseus near the water, I'll drive down Lake Hudson way and have a look."

I drove to Lake Hudson, circled it on three sides, but saw no signs of Max, no dogs at all. Then I parked the station wagon and walked along the familiar bike path leading to Newark—a path Max and I had often traveled—I walked three or four miles of bike path, but found no Circe, no dogs, no Max.

Thursday went much as Wednesday, no signs of Max, although in pre-dawn I could have sworn I heard Circe's yip-yip-yip and pack-dog barking from the valley beyond Robinson's woods.

Friday afternoon after classes I was ready to continue the campus search when the phone rang. It was Tom Waters of the Denison Development Office. He said he'd come to the field house for his over-lunch-hour workout and swim, and had been told there was a black and tan hound hung up in the steel spike fence beside the entryway turnstile. One of the fieldhouse janitors had seen the dog get trapped. This black and tan was running with a whitish female, a smaller, slender dog. She has sifted through the steel fence and the hound had tried the same maneuver running at full speed, had got only his head and chest through, had been stopped halfway to glory.

"After swimming I went to see the dog," Tom Waters said. "I'm just about sure it's your Max."

"Is he—he isn't dead, is he?"

"No, but he's caught—locked in—in this unbelievably tight space, and he appears to have barked himself out. He's rubbed off fur where his haunches hold him. To tell you the truth I didn't get real close; he seems pretty desperate. I thought I'd better call you."

"Right! Thanks, Tom. I'll be there pronto."

As I pulled off the main campus road leading to the athletic facility I saw Tom Waters waiting. Then I caught sight of Max, wedged between reddish wrought-steel posts some ten feet to the right of the turnstile. Judging by his off-key barking, the length of exposed tongue, the lather on his neck and shoulders that I could see as I ran toward him, he'd gone mad during his ordeal. Still he was doing his damnedest to move his body—lunging backward and forward—anything to disengage the steel jaws that had closed upon him when in the feverish excitement of keeping close to Circe he had driven himself halfway through the five inch opening.

"Max, it's Poppa," I cried as I got to him, knelt beside him. I caught his head and held him steady. Slowly the frantic brown eyes took on a thank-God-you're-here glow. "I thought I'd better call you—just in case he was biting mad," Tom Waters said.

"Right, Tom! He may be biting mad, but he's still Max." I was working my fingers from his neck to his chest and haunches where flesh showed as though scalded. "Now to get you out of here, old boy."

"Maybe I should help from the back—the other side," Tom Waters said. "Just in case he has a mind to snap." He stepped through the turnstile and approached Max from the rear. "Do we go forward or back? God, he's wedged tight."

Sliding my fingers between the steel spikes and trembling ribs, doing my best to take off the terrible pressure, I said, "I think we'd better work the head and chest back through. We know they had to get pushed through that space to get him into this fix." To Max I murmured: "Steady boy, steady. If and when you're—" His look stopped me, but I added, "Okay fella, but you can see the mess you've got yourself into."

Lowering my hands, fingers taking his body weight off his front legs, I managed to lift him clear of the ground—to stretch out his head and chest as far as possible. Tom Waters was lifting and pulling gently on the haunches, but we were getting nowhere.

Tom Waters muttered: "Maybe we ought to call the Fire Department. Have somebody with a welding torch cut the damned wrought steel."

"Let's try again," I said. "You hold the haunches down this time, I'll lift his head and chest." To Max, I said: "Come on, Maxie, give us your best." Again I lifted the seventy-five pound body by head and neck, and pushed, pushed hard. No soap! "Max," I said, "if you would tell us exactly how you got yourself into this pickle we might be able to get you out."

Max looked up at me with pleading in his eyes. Then

his gaze hardened, as if to say: Get on with it, get on with it. Break my bones, if you must.

Tom Waters spoke: "The janitor said the white bitch just slipped through the spikes like a hand in a shirt sleeve."

"She would," I said. "Max, you're a large male fist in this steel shirt sleeve. Think of yourself that way and do it!" To Tom I added: "Let's give it one more go!"

Max, as if he sensed necessity beyond means, elongated his head and neck, and I pushed on both, one hand on each. Tom Waters pulled on the back legs, laid himself back and pulled. "A little more," he breathed, "a little more!"

Suddenly Max's body gave a surge backwards—whooshed!—cleared the steel spikes and he tumbled free and lay on the ground, trembling and shaken. I stepped through the turnstile and knelt beside him. He began gingerly exploring his ribs and chest, his haunches, as if to ask why they failed him, and ended up licking my hand.

"He seems to have damaged his chest," Tom Waters said. "His breathing?"

"He was once kneed in the chest, had his ribs cracked," I said. I was massaging his head, his ears, feeling the little diamond of heat return to the domed head.

"You think he'll be all right?" Tom Waters said. "I could help you carry him to the station wagon."

"Oh, he'll be all right. He's a tough old hound. It may take a bit of time," I said, "but he'll be all right and able to walk. You'd better be getting up to the Development Office in case some rich alumnus wishes to donate another Max trap. Thanks a whole lot, Tom. And let me know if ever you need a hand. I really owe you one."

"You're sure he'll be okay?" Tom Waters repeated.

"He'll be okay," I said. "I'll just let him rest a little and then I'll get him into his bus.

Goodbye Heart

My blithe assurance—was it arrogance—to Tom Waters was to come back to haunt me, haunts me to this day, for Max was not all right. Because our veterinarian friend Dr. William Sanders in Alexandria had retired from his practice, we had to find Max a new doctor and it took some time to find someone reputed to be competent, and to set up an appointment. The new young doctor—Elmer Perkins Probo—examined Max in his immaculate clinic on Reagan Avenue and pronounced him in excellent health, none the worse for his three-day marathon Circe-run, his losing bout with Denison's wrought iron fence.

When I informed Dr. Probo that Max passed blood right after the fence ordeal, and went through a stage of what seemed to my untrained ear to be irregular heartbeats, that he had not resumed eating and appeared to be losing weight, Dr. Probo assured me his temperature was normal, his eyes clear, his coat sleek, and it was well for a dog nearing the end of his twelfth year of life not to be overweight.

"A large dog at age twelve is the equivalent of a man in

his early eighties." Dr. Probo said. "Now you just take him home and give him a bit of LTC—Loving Tender Care—and in no time at all he'll be the dog you've owned these many years. Here, I'll lift him off the table."

"Thanks," I said, "I'll manage."

Max had listened to our exchange with his eyes fixed on my face as if he wanted to inquire about such strange language: *loving tender care, owned.* Now he wriggled his way into my arms, kissed my cheek, and slid to the floor. He held his head for me to snap on his leather leash, and casting a wary eye toward Dr. Probo who was busy dictating charges to a young woman at a computer, he strode out to his bus.

When I explained to Jeanne the cursory nature of Dr. Probo's examination of Max, his rosy prediction, she said: "Any doctor who has the gall to tell you to give Max TLC and translate it for you—well, such a doctor is not to be trusted. I'd get a second opinion, the sooner the better."

"Dr. Probo said he should probably see Max again in seven or eight weeks," I said. "I'm to call for an appointment after the holidays."

"So he can tell you to give Max LTC? Any doctor who is that lacking in the power of observation—" Jeanne shook her head, but went on, "Max appears to be sick. Look at his body shape, his lethargy. He's taken to drinking more water than usual—"

"I told Dr. Probo all that."

"He eats almost nothing," Jeanne said. "And still his stomach appears swollen."

"He doesn't complain," I said.

"He wouldn't complain if he were dying, and you know

it." Jeanne said. "He'd be fearful he was hurting us. He has definitely aged and—well, I'd get a second opinion."

We were in the living room as we talked. Jeanne was seated on the sofa, I sat in my favorite chair. Max, who had been lying in the kitchen, heard his name being repeated and entered the room. When he got to the sofa he gave Jeanne a nudge on the arm. He stopped and glanced toward me, then strode around the sofa, passed between it and the coffee table, and lay his chin on my knee, gave me a gentle shove.

"He's putting in his two cents worth," I said. "Speaking his mind."

"He's agreeing with me. Get a second doctor's opinion, eh, Max?"

Still resting his chin on my knee, Max raised his eyes to my face, permitting their whites to show.

I held out my hand, gently rubbed behind the silky hairs of his ear. "That does it: we see a second doctor."

Finding a second veterinarian and setting up the appointment took six days. In the meantime Max's health continued to deteriorate. Dr. Huston Wellsley was an older man who had just moved his practice to Licking County, and as soon as Max and I entered his modest office I sensed that he cared about dogs. As I lifted Max to the examination table—Max always made lifting him easy by stepping upward into my arms—Dr. Wellsley was recording answers to his questions: Max's history, his age, weight, the reason for our visit

He turned and spoke to Max: "Max, old fella, I see

you've gone gray in the chops, and you do appear a trifle bloated, your shoulders and legs a bit emaciated." As he spoke he fondled Max's ears, ran his hands the length of the body, and deftly inserted a thermometer. A moment later he said: "His temperature's off just a bit."

When I explained that I sensed by laying my ear to Max's chest that his heart rate was at times irregular, Dr. Wellsley nodded. Instead of asking me how I knew I could judge a heart rate by ear, as Dr. Probo had done, Dr. Wellsley laid his stethoscope to Max's chest, moved it here and there, listening. "Well," he said, "his heart rate is normal today, but let's run a blood sample and test for heart worm."

No sooner said than done—the rubber tourniquet on front leg, the blood sample drawn. A couple minutes later while Max and I talked about vets and their work, Dr. Wellsley looked up from his microscope and assured me that Max was not afflicted with heart worm. He went on: "But I just don't like his overall appearance." He laid his hand under Max's chin and drew him to his feet. Inserting a finger at dewlap he looked at Max's gums. "Something's not right here," he said, frowning. He held out the lip for me to see. "That white bloodless condition—there's something really off here."

Max turned his head and sneezed. Dr. Wellsley chuckled. "Gesundheit, polite fella." Again he slid Max to his side and began exploring his neck and shoulders and abdomen. He looked up and asked if Max might have been injured sometime in the chest and/or the stomach.

At mention of Randy Neighbor's knee to Max's chest years ago, he nodded. And when I told of Max's recent ordeal at the wrought-iron trap at Denison he nodded again, as if his hands were confirming what his ears heard. Finally he said, "You said Max weighed seventy-five?"

"Let's just check that out," Dr. Wellsley said. He swept Max into his arms, talking softly to him, and stepped across to the scale. He set Max back on the examination table and again stepped on the scale to check his own weight. "I get sixty-three pounds." As he spoke his hands were exploring Max's body—chest and abdomen. In a minute he said: "Lay your hand right here. Feel this."

I did as he said. My hand encountered a lump that now it was pinned in place within the abdomen seemed the size of a baseball, or larger. "What is it?" I asked.

"Tumor—a growth on the spleen or liver."

"Is it—could you operate?"

Dr. Wellsley had straightened and was jotting something on Max's examination sheet. He laid his hand on Max's head and looked me in the eye. "I could but—he's going on twelve?"

"He'll be twelve next week. December 15."

"Then I'd advise against an operation. We'd be sure to cause him pain with very little chance of his recovering his health, very little chance of prolonging his life—any normal life."

I held Max's body to my chest as the words hit home. What he understood of the words I don't know. But he shifted his head to mouth my hands. Maybe he was saying it was time to leave the examination. Maybe he was saying it would be all right.

Dr. Wellsley did not send me off with pompous mouthing that I treat Max with TLC. His counsel ran to a bottle of vitamin-mineral supplement, which he handed me and the suggestion that I try Max on a diet rich in liver, chicken, eggs, custard, noodles, even the so-called forbidden whole milk. "Feed plenty of protein," he said. "In fact, just feed anything you think he'd fancy, anything he can be got to eat."

"Is it that dire?" I asked, thinking of last suppers.

"Well," Dr. Wellsley looked at Max who was shifting his eyes from face to face as we spoke, "you can never tell about these hounds. They're as tough as case-hardened nails, but you and your wife have to be ready for just about any eventuality." He reached out and ran a finger from Max's forehead to his nose. "Max, I've got to tell you you're the best patient I've had today. That's no shit! And I've had twenty or twenty-five animals on that table today." He looked away, cleared his throat and then spoke to me:

"Now you take care. You, your wife, and Max."

Max got to his feet. My ears were brushing his ears, and I was aware of speaking across keen umbrella antennae that knew the word *Jeanne*. "I was wondering about her. Telling her won't be easy."

Dr. Wellsley faced me again. "She'll need to know—but that's just it. None of us can ever really know."

"Is he—" I nodded above Max, "is he in any pain? Is it likely to get impossibly painful? We wouldn't want that."

"I can't say for sure, but I think not—hope not. You call me if you—should you think I'm needed. I'll be available even if I'm not scheduled in office. My home phone is in the book."

"Thank you," I said. "I appreciate this. Here Maxie." I lifted Max from the table, stooped to hook up his leather leash, and we went to his bus.

Our visit to Dr. Wellsley took place on December 7, one week and one day before Max's twelfth birthday. A calendar date that in its 1941 import burns forever in the memory of all Americans of our generation. Forewarned, and aware of what was taking place with each hour's passing. Jeanne and I accepted each hour, each minute with Max, as the bounty it was. For his part, Max seemed equally aware that every day, every sunrise, every sunset, had grown precious beyond telling.

In his nightly habit of running off to his toilet and then coming back past the kitchen window where Jeanne prepared our supper and I prepared his special bowl of liver or noodles or custard, he set his umbrella ears dancing and then turned his head at precisely the right moment to catch our eyes—to say I know what you're doing for me, and I thank you for it. Once he had eaten whatever slight portion of the meal he could eat, he made it a ritual to come by to give Jeanne and me each a thank-you nudge before settling in the corner of his couch or in his favorite spot between our chairs.

When one afternoon I went to the garden to spade in the last of the over one hundred bags of leaves Jeanne had raked from under our neighbors' maples, our annual late winter rite, the final laying to sleep of the garden, Max stayed close by my side. He made it a point to stand among the leaves as I shook them out, whirl round and round in them, drop down and mouth and throw them, restore and sustain this garden, this bit of good earth we had tended.

When Jeanne took him on his morning and afternoon walks—a daily ritual—he became very definite in choosing his path, how far he walked, and where he stopped. As his strength gradually failed him, he would stop and stare into the distance, probing time and space. The times that Jeanne and I walked him together and beheld him standing so, we could not keep from wondering whether he was reading a future we could not comprehend. Standing and staring, was he not asking whether he was to meet his mother, his sisters, his brothers, his old friend Wolfgang. Or perhaps at some future time that he comprehended and beheld: Jeanne and me, Chief Leaping Bear, Blue Star, Polly Edwards, his many friends?

During our long evenings, as Jeanne and I sat by the brightest lamp reading, Max now took to leaving his sofa to settle at our feet. He would drop to the floor a little distance away, then scooch forward until his body was touching the two of us, our feet, our legs. Linking by touch the three of us. So his birthday came and passed, and the old year stumbled to its close. Now his behavior became so unusual, so valedictory in its nuances, that I had to say to Jeanne: "As sure as the sun moves in the sky, he knows."

"Of course he knows," Jeanne said. "He has a large soul. He's telling us in every way he can that he knows and cares." She paused then went on: "But that's been his way all his life. You know he must find something odd about us. We were here when he came, apparently we're to be here when he goes—" Her voice broke. "Almost eternal to him. Somewhat omniscient—the way you'd show up with his bus."

"I hope to God he's found us equal to his trust," I said. "What a guy! How did Harvey Roundsdale put it that day at the IGA: 'He's some dog, some dog!'"

Forewarned, and aware of what was occurring with every hour's passing still Jeanne and I were in no way ready for what befell on January 8, the day Max died. That Sunday began quite normally, with Max getting Jeanne and me underway, waking us with a gentle nudge and two-note greeting. After breakfast he walked me to the station wagon and climbed in for our usual drive to Taylor's Drug Store where we bought the New York *Times*. Once we secured the *Times* we drove down to the Granville-Newark bike path where we often went for Sunday morning walks.

This time Max went slowly along the macadam path, only a hundred yards or so. But as he went he paused often to look up at me: Remember this! When I told him he had done well, we could go back anytime, he stopped and gave the path ahead his long stare. Place, space and time.

When I spoke to him again, to ask if he were ready to go back to his bus, he looked up and set his tail in motion—performed a little antic dance that took him off the path, where he picked up a stick. Now he turned and headed to the station wagon, holding his cigar at a jaunty angle, the whites of his eyes showing. At the car door he held out the stick, a Maxish offering, approbation of the path, all it was.

Arriving home he headed to his feed bowl in the kitchen. With gusto he devoured the bowl of dinner he had ignored the night before. His choke chain clanking against earthen bowl as he moved, he licked the bowl clean, left it shining. Then he turned and drank deeply from his water pan. Thoroughly replenished he strode into the living room and climbed onto his sofa, his head laid on the sofa arm so he could keep an eye on Jeanne and me as we settled with the *Times,* passed parts of it back and forth.

Except for an afternoon jaunt to his toilet, he stayed on his sofa throughout the day. About 8 o'clock that night he got down from the sofa and went to Jeanne, who was engaged in working the *Times'* crossword puzzle. He gave her a nudge, rested his head on her knee, and then came to me and did the same.

"I think he wants to go out," Jeanne said.

I opened the back door and held it as he went gingerly down the steps. Once on the patio he appeared to suffer a slight stroke: his body wavered, his legs gave way and he fell. It was cold—a low cloud of rain touched the earth—so while Jeanne held the door I gathered him in my arms and carried him in and placed him just inside the door where we covered him with sweaters.

He was breathing with difficulty, but he dozed off. In his sleep he dreamed, his legs moving, his tail giving several fitful wags. About 10 o'clock he awakened and got to his feet, stood by the door. As soon as I got the door open he moved down the steps but his legs went out of control This time he collapsed on a pile of maple leaves Jeanne had left for winter mulch on the roots of the rhododendrons at the back of the house. I knelt by him, spoke to him. I felt his head rise, his nose touch my hand. Again Jeanne held the door as I gathered him in my arms and carried him inside—to the kitchen. Jeanne spread old sweaters and wool shirts I had worn in gardening and I laid him on them.

He was having difficulty in breathing, and sensing a reckoning beyond our ken, Jeanne and I settled down on the floor, with him between us. His breathing increased to panting, gasping for every breath. We touched him and talked to him, telling him things would be all right—that he could just relax, that we would take care.

For ten or so minutes he lay there, breathing with great difficulty, saliva forming on his lips. Two or three times he fought for control, raising his head to fix his eyes on Jeanne or me, touching for an instant a caressing hand. Then his body trembled and his breathing stopped. There was a silence, a silence so absolute it seemed everlasting. Jeanne and I looked at one another, our eyes blurring.

Later, when we could see again, we touched for one last time his domed head, his silky ears, his ruff, his chest. I closed his eyes and we covered him over.

On Monday I awakened before daylight. Cold but thawing rain had fallen during the early morning hours. As soon as I could see my tools I dug a grave on the bank above Jeanne's uppermost flower bed. A site that overlooked the house, the orchard, the garden, the beech woods. No sun rose but when it was fully light Jeanne and I carried him out and laid him in his grave on a white sheet we had spread. We were scarcely equal to what we had to do, but we did it. Jeanne looked long on the sweet domed head, the silky ears, the sleek black body. I folded the sheet in place across the body. Jeanne shaped a tepee of hands as Chief Leaping Bear had done so long ago. I filled the grave, tamped the earth, relaid the sod. Our lives would never be the same. Max was home.

Tale of a Waggish Dog

The Tale of A Waggish Dog
can be purchased through your local bookstore
or through

Mayhaven Publishing
P O Box 557
Mahomet, IL 61853

Other books by Paul Bennett can be purchased through:
Denison University Bookstore
Denison University
Granville, OH 43023

Other Books by Mayhaven Publishing

Tangled Tassels: Tales of Academe
Richard Eastman

95 Years with John "Jack" Day
John "Jack" Day

Ten Sisters: A True Story
Authored by the Ten Sisters

Dear Family
A Family Saga Through Letters, Diaries and Personal Stories
Marjorie Lynn

Abraham Lincoln: From Skeptic to Prophet
Wayne C. Temple

Long Story Short
Nancy Easter Shick

On the Wings of Love
Donna Rhodes Collins

Gardens of the Streets
William Lewis Clark